anonymous

formatted by liberty under attack
publications

◼ LIBERTY UNDER ATTACK
◼ PUBLICATIONS *tell your story*

Looking for your next read or listen?

1. **Adventures in Illinois Law: Witnessing Tyranny Firsthand** by Shane Radliff (Audiobook/Anthology)
2. **Adventures in Illinois Higher Education: Communist Indoctrination** by Shane Radliff (Audiobook/Anthology)
3. **An Illusive Phantom of Hope: A Critique of Reformism** by Kyle Rearden (Audiobook/Anthology)
4. **The Production of Security** by Gustave de Molinari (Audiobook)
5. **Are Cops Constitutional?** by Roger Roots (Audiobook)
6. **Vonu: The Search for Personal Freedom** by Rayo (Audiobook)
7. **Argumentation Ethics: An Anthology** by Hans-Herman Hoppe et al (Anthology)
8. **Just Below The Surface: A Guide to Security Culture** by Kyle Rearden (Audiobook/Anthology)
9. **Sedition, Subversion, and Sabotage, Field Manual No. 1: A Three Part Solution to the State** by Ben Stone (Audiobook)
10. **#agora** by anonymous (Paperback and Kindle)
11. **Vonu: A Strategy for Self-Liberation** by Shane Radliff (Paperback/Audiobook)
12. **Second Realm: Book on Strategy** by Smuggler and XYZ (Paperback)
13. **Vonu: The Search for Personal Freedom** by Rayo (Special Paperback Reprint/Audiobook)
14. **Vonu: The Search for Personal Freedom, Part 2 [Letters From Rayo]** (Paperback)
15. **Going Mobile** by Tom Marshall (Paperback/Audiobook)
16. **Anarchist to Abolitionist: A Bad Quaker's Journey** by Ben Stone
17. **Brushfire, A Thriller** by Matthew Wojtecki

Copyright Notice and Publisher's Note

Publisher's Note

The following novella was originally found at Anarplex.net and has no author attributed to it. We here at *LUA Publications* found the book highly valuable and decided to format it digitally and also put it in physical print. That's said, we are not responsible for this incredible story you are about to read; all credit goes to "Anonymous," whoever that may be.

"Our strategy for liberty is the creation of a culture of liberty, a society that occupies its own protected space and implements independent systems of cooperation. We need to create a Second Realm."

–Smuggler and XYZ, *Second Realm: Book on Strategy*

BitCoin
========

"Dude, check this out", Tom says. He puts his laptop on my chest. I try to get up on my mattress without pushing the laptop to the floor.

"What the fuck", I say, "I'm sleeping."

"You'll shit bricks when you see this", Tom says.
I grab the laptop, then blink my eyes to lose the sleep. It's a website.

www.bitcoin.org - BitCoin P2P Virtual Currency

"What is this?", I ask.

"Dude, it's a crypto-currency!"

"A what?"

"A digital currency. You can send me money and I don't know your real name. Or your account number. And nobody else does, either."

"Why would I send you money?"

"That's not the point. I could make an online store, accepting BitCoins, and I wouldn't have to pay taxes."

"What? Wouldn't the government just take a third of your BitCoins?"

"They would, I bet. But how are they going to find out how many BitCoins I have?"

My thinking isn't straight yet. I get up and walk to the shower.

"Ew, put some clothes on, man!", Tom shouts after me.

"Don't wake me, you fuckknuckle", I say. But my voice is still kind of sleepy and he can't hear me. And he's reading the stupid website, not listening.

***

After I shower, I sit down on the sofa in the kitchen to have some breakfast.

"This is excellent", Tom says, sitting down and putting the laptop on the table.

"Your mom is excellent", I mumble, mouth full of eggs and bacon. He ignores me.

"If I can set up a website anonymously, they won't even know who is selling stuff. And they won't find out through the payment system, because it is anonymous."

"Who's going to pay you with BitCoins?", I ask.

Tom thinks for a second.

"That's a good point", he says. He thinks more.

"Everyone who doesn't want to pay taxes, I guess", he says.

"And every drug dealer, kidnapper, hit man and child pornographer who doesn't want to get caught!", I say.

He shrugs.

***

"You see, the fiat monetary system imposed upon us by the different governments is about to collapse", Tom says.

I nod, mostly because I don't have anything to say.

"They've been printing money and inflating the M3 like crazy. Did you know that the amount of dollars has DOUBLED in the last five years?"

"I did not know that."

"Right! Nobody knows that! At least not the majority of people. And the Euro isn't much better off - if it is better off at all. The amount of euros has doubled in the last 11 years. All governments are in massive debt. The US are approaching 15 trillion dollars in federal debt. Not including states, cities, municipalities.."

"Yea, yea, I get it. So how's this BitThing going to help?"

"BitCoin", he says, "Well: it can't be inflated beyond a certain point."

"What do you mean?"

"What the central banks do is print more money, not really print it necessarily, but create more electronic money. That can't be done beyond a certain point in BitCoin."

"But isn't it purely electronic? Why couldn't I just print billions of new BitCoins?"

"There's a built in security check. All the computers on the network constantly check every transaction and the validity of every coin created. That means in order to create one fake BitCoin, you'd have to beat the computational power of the whole network."

"If they can print dollars and euros, why wouldn't they just do that instead?"

"Are you kidding?", Tom looks incredulous, "That's hundreds of thousands of machines to beat. Maybe millions. And the number is growing. See? I just joined."

He shows me the BitCoin app. It says he has zero BitCoins, worth around zero euros.

"So you think people are going to use this and evade taxes?"

"Fuck yes. Who wants to pay taxes?", he says.

"But then the government won't have any money", I say.

"Exactly", Tom says.

"But the government would go bankrupt. It would collapse."

Tom doesn't say anything.

"But wouldn't that be anarchy?", I ask.

Tom grins.

***

"But the government wouldn't let this happen", I say, "I don't think they WANT to go bankrupt."

"What the government wants or doesn't want won't matter. You can't cheat math. They have so much debt, it realistically can never be paid back. They'd have to cut 90% of government spending for years. Even if they wanted to do it, they couldn't. And in effect, this would mean anarchy, too. If the government stops 90% of all its activities, these fields will be picked up by private entrepreneurs. So even if they do it, and repay all the debt, they wouldn't really be a government any longer."

Tom is really into this whole collapse thing.

"So what are they going to do?"

"There's several things they could do. First, just default on the debt."

"Default?"

"They could just say 'We won't pay it back, fuck you.', and never pay it back."

"But that would be theft."

Tom laughs.

"Everything they do is based on theft, why would they care?", he says.

"Good point", I say, "what are the other options?"

"They could inflate the money supply even more. You see, when they weaken the currency with their money printing, they also make their own debt less valuable. Would you rather pay back 100€ worth 100€ or would you rather pay back 100€ worth 10€?"

"10€", I say.

"Exactly. If the money is worth less at the time they pay it back, they save money. That's why they inflate so much. But it can't go on forever."

"Why not?"

"Remember the Weimar Republic?"

"Yea. You mean we'll use wheelbarrows to buy stuff?"

"That is one option. Hyperinflation. Once a loaf of bread costs five million euros, they'll pay back their now-worthless debt and be debt free. Of course, the currency is destroyed."

"Then they'll have to make a new currency", I say.

"Right. And repeat the whole thing in 50 years, like last time. Or..", he stops.

"Or what?"

"Or, maybe, this time, there will be another currency already in place. One that isn't controlled by central banks. That can't be hyper-inflated."

"BitCash?", I say.

"BitCoin, you moron", he says. I giggle.

"What if they shut BitCoin down?"

"First, that wouldn't be easy. They'd have to control virtually every computer out there. They can't just block the Internet, you know. Trillions of dollars and euros are traded over the Internet. Second, BitCoin isn't necessarily the only DC available."

"DC?"

"Digital Currency", Tom says, "don't you know anything?"

"Apparently not", I say.

"So there could be several DCs at the same time. Some people might prefer currencies based on gold. Some on silver. Or something completely different. It will be very difficult for government to prevent the use of a DC once it is commonly accepted. Like it's impossible to prevent file sharing, even though it's technically illegal."

"But then I'll have to carry over 9000 different currencies in my pocket, every shop will use its own money!"

"Don't be silly. Nobody would want that, so it wouldn't happen", Tom says.

He clicks around on his laptop.

"I've sent you a pdf you should read. It explains the whole thing in much greater detail", he says.

I decide to go back to bed and sleep some more.

***

I open Tom's email. Attached is a pdf:

A Lodging of Wayfaring Men - by Anonymous

I start reading. It's a novel about some guys building a digital currency. They hide it inside of a online computer game. They call it "Gamma". Eventually, this leads the FBI on their track, but they're never caught. It's kind of open ended, but it seems to end very well for the guys and not so well for the government.

There's also a bunch of religious stuff in the book. People cry a lot and hug and confess their deepest secrets to each other. I guess this novel was really personal for the author, Anonymous. I wonder if that is really his name. Haha.

After looking around online for "a lodging of wayfaring men", I find a copy of the pdf online. It is hosted on a strange website:

anarplex.net

"Anarplex is the operator of GammaDX and a provider of darknet services for various crypto-tribes and Phyles. Our mission is to create a home for tribes-people, their affiliates and associates by providing superior communications and processing services."

So GammaDX, hu? Like Gamma in the book?

When I check the hosted pdf, it isn't signed "Anonymous" but "Paul Rosenberg". I write the name down. Then I check the site some more.

There are some more pdfs to download and instructions on how to join an IRC channel:

Server: agora.anarplex.net

Port: 14716
Channel: #anarplex (we are the ops)
SSL is required

I download an IRC client and connect to the channel.

#agora
======

*You have joined #agora
guest004: hello anyone here
bill: Hello
Denton: hi guest
Hiro: hi
c4ty: hi
guest004: what is this place?
Denton: how did you get here?
Hiro: its an irc channel, duh
c4ty: its for cyber sex asl
Bill: This is the last resort for freedom loving people.
guest004: i read a lodging for wayfaring men and then found the website
Denton: anarplex.net?
guest004: yes
c4ty: you can change your name with "/nick moron"
*guest004 changed name to c4ty_is_a_moron
c4ty_is_a_moron: like this?
c4ty: very funny moron
*c4ty_is_a_moron changed name to daniel
(private message) Denton: are u from germany?
(private message) daniel: how do you know?
(private message) Denton: your IP and provider
(private message) daniel: oh ok where are you from?
(private message) Denton: berlin :)
(private message) daniel: berlin berlin! many ancaps there?
(private message) Denton: some. not "many", but a few.
(private message) Denton: probably more than anywere else in germany
(private message) daniel: cool i'll visit u one day
(private message) Denton: sure :-) ur welcome any time
Denton: did u read second realm strategy?
daniel: no whats that
Denton: a strategy book. like a practical follow up to lodging.
c4ty: denton thinks its the bomb! his favourite book.
Denton: https://anarplex.net/hosted/files/second-realm-strategy.pdf
daniel: thx i'll check it out

daniel: c4ty: how did you like it
c4ty: SR? not too bad
Denton: haha, she lives by it. its her bible.
c4ty: shut up denton. i should kick you.
Denton: im the op
c4ty: like i care!!1
daniel: caty: where are you from
c4ty: berlin
daniel: every1 is from berlin. whats so great about berlin?
c4ty: everything
daniel: ill check out this SR book
daniel: cu guys
*You have left #agora

I download the Second Realm Strategy book.

The Second Realm
Book on Strategy
Crypto-Anarchy, Tradecraft, TAZ, and Counterculture

It's quite short, like 70 pages. There are three parts. First, an overview of
the situation, obstacles, and possibilities. Second, technical solutions to
create a Second Realm. Third, the culture needed to create and sustain such
a Second Realm.

"Anyone subscribing to a radical philosophy of liberty, must face the
pressing question of how to progress from our current condition of
insufficient liberty, to a society where individual liberty is respected."

They call the current society the "First Realm". The First Realm is ruled by
politicians, personal freedoms are inhibited and restrained. Rather than
advocating a revolution, they want to build a "Second Realm", one that is
free from the rulers of the First Realm. More and more parts of our lives
can be transferred to the Second Realm, until an individual lives mostly
free in the Second Realm, while being technically ruled over in the First
Realm. One day, the First Realm rulers may lose their power, due to
everyone joining the Second Realm.

Technically, the Second Realm is described as encrypted communication,
encrypted currencies, anonymous and pseudonymous identities, and
untraceable action. Like Neo in the Matrix: by day, he's just a computer
programmer. By night, he's an expert hacker. Only in the Second Realm,
nobody will find the connection between the two. Or so they say.

I could be my usual self in the First Realm, pay some taxes, pretend to have a normal job and be an ordinary citizen. In the Second Realm, I could be free. Do whatever I want.

This not only sounds like freedom, it sounds like adventure. I send Tom the link to the Second Realm pdf.

Then I look up how to get encrypted emails. I make a private and public PGP key and send the public one to Tom. Only when the sender uses my public key and I use my private key can the email be read. For anyone else, it's just unintelligible garbage:

qANQR1DBwEwD4PSJmhZ2mJoBB/oDkeTMBP+qTZCbrH0x+ltec/FpC
wYLrojTKR4O
he1qjeJshaR5j6B0tpYeLGiRf/4OfkKNNDCmRjkT9ofRCgv5GO9sz6WO
eZiMWhjU
hT1LF8K84xLvCeXPIwdFNThF3vFktuMTy1fDfl/nFDSjXsigD/3mmbH
mN0S9bbUE
XfEaceWPSiHqIZME9Mr57LeySCag2LVBtAVFN4+aMRH9q/YDB4KK
XlUcmIR4z64K
WU4fFpdQ7Bp30JCi4L/1R3d9AQgnhdgnv253yYJ1qS+XcVxCcXVEHa
ChcfUcoNWs

I also get a plugin for my email program, so I can send and receive encrypted mails comfortably. I'm itching to send loads of encrypted mails, but I don't know to whom, or what to send, so I return to #agora.

*You have joined #agora
daniel: hi again
bill: Welcome back! How are you?
daniel: im fine how about you
bill: I'm alright.
daniel: whats up
Denton: up is the direction pointing away from source of gravity
bill: lol
Michael: lol
Hiro: lol
FellowTraveler: rofl
daniel: haha i mean whats going on
daniel: hello?
daniel: wheres c4ty
Hiro: probably out trading
daniel: trading what?
Hiro: how would i know what she trades? money, i'm guessing

daniel: ???
Denton: i told u she lives by the book :)
daniel: so r u guys using bitcoin?
FellowTraveler: bitcoin is for amateurs
daniel: im an amateur
FellowTraveler: i wouldn't have guessed.
Hiro: i use bitcoin sometimes
Hiro: do you want some bitcoins to try it out?
daniel: sure how can i make an account
Hiro: go to mybitcoin.com or download the client

I open the browser and make a free account on mybitcoin.com. It's pretty simple and I get a hash of my adress that I'm supposed to give to other people:

Account Balance is: 0.00 BTC (0.00 USD @ 0.3229)

Your Bitcoin Payment Address is:
15H21NBVokRPwd41pSjVxed7dEjo3sM55m

I go back to IRC.

daniel: my bc adress is 15H21NBVokRPwd41pSjVxed7dEjo3sM55m
Hiro: k i sent you some
Denton: me2
bill: Oh yea! It's BitCoin time! Dump him!
FellowTraveler: bitcoin isnt that great
daniel: how long till the bitcoins arrive on my account?
Hiro: could be a few minutes. usually less than 10 minutes.
FellowTraveler: it has to traverse the P2P network
daniel: ok
daniel: FT: what do u recommend
Hiro: OT
bill: OT
Denton: OT
FellowTraveler: OpenTransactions
daniel: lol
Hiro: only there's no client yet
Denton: and no running server
bill: And no mint.
daniel: whats a mint
bill: An entity that creates a currency. Like minting coins.
daniel: i see

I switch and check my BitCoin account.

Account Balance is: 35.36 BTC (11.42 USD @ 0.3229)

daniel: so 1 bc = $0.3
bill: At the moment, yes. It fluctuates, like all currencies.
daniel: which way does it fluctuate
bill: Both. But it has generally risen. It used to be only a few cents.
daniel: nice thx 4 the money guys haha :D
Hiro: sure
bill: You're welcome.
(private message) FellowTraveler: seriously though, check out OT
(private message) daniel: sure whats the url
(private message) FellowTraveler:
https://github.com/FellowTraveler/Open-Transactions/

I go to the site and it gives me a description and a list of files:

"Transaction processor featuring Untraceable Digital Cash, Anonymous
Numbered Accounts, Triple-Signed Receipts, Basket Currencies, and
Signed XML Contracts. Also supports cheques, invoices, payment plans,
markets with trades, and other instruments... it's like PGP for Money....
Uses OpenSSL and Lucre blinded tokens. ---Mac OS X, Linux, FreeBSD,
Android, Windows---Native APIs for Java, Ruby, Python, PHP, Perl, C,
C++, Objective-C, C#, Tcl, and LISP."

I click on "README".

"WHAT IS Open Transactions?

It's a solid, easy-to-use, FINANCIAL CRYPTO and DIGITAL CASH
LIBRARY. Including an operational API, SERVER and CLIENT."

Sounds a lot like the Gamma-software from A Lodging of Wayfaring Men.
Or BitCoin, just more advanced.

(private message) daniel: looks cool
(private message) FellowTraveler: yea unfortunately not too much users
yet
(private message) daniel: why
(private message) FellowTraveler: for one there's no way to use it yet. no
client like mybitcoin.com or similar.
(private message) daniel: how difficult is it to make one

(private message) FellowTraveler: not too difficult. the API is almost finished and is public. go to the API site.

I check the API out. There's a list of functions to call and wrappers for several programming languages. In fact, most programming languages I know are covered. I click on "The Road Forward":

"..Integrate this software with as many legitimate entities as possible. Such as community currencies and LETS systems. Make transaction processors a normal part of the Internet with many legitimate uses and users.

..Integrate with as many profitable entities as possible. Such as Tor banks, online casinos, and any other online business that benefits from offering anonymity to their customers. Find specific niches where the software adds value now. Let the money drive it.

..Integrate with anonymous networks. Networks such as Tor, I2P, Freenet, etc could all benefit from an anonymous payment mechanism. Open Transactions wallet software should also be a file-sharing client and node for anonymous networks. They should be one and the same.

..Android client, Windows client, iPhone client, iPad client, Java client, Mac OSX client

..High-level interfaces for developers. (Almost done with C++ and Java.) Build this library into a multitude of different software apps.

..Integrate with popular Wordpress payment processing plugins. So the Internet can become digital-cash enabled overnight

..Integrate with Anonymous Remailers, Nym Servers, and other projects that would benefit.

..Get a network of servers up and operating, as well as a bunch of different issuers, so that the first real basket currencies can be issued."

I go back to IRC.

(private message) daniel: so lets make a client
(private message) FellowTraveler: sure. have a look at the API. any questions, just ask me. ill help you out for sure.
(private message) daniel: cool. ill try it out.
*You have left #agora

I fire up TextMate and bookmark the API site.

Caty

I exit the ICE bullet train and take a look at the big clock hanging in the central hall of the station. I'm right on time. Even though it's already dark, I can feel a warm summer breeze going through the building. Hesitantly, I make my first step to the left.

"Hey dumbass, where are you going?", I hear a girl saying behind me. I turn around slowly.

There she is.

Taller than I expected, though not really tall. Her matte black pony tail whips up and down with each step as she comes closer. Her eyes are big and brown and rimmed by ludicrous amounts of that black stuff that girls use to make their eyes look bigger. It works. There is a small metal ring in the right wing of her nose. On the left side of her head, where plenty of black hair has escaped from her pony tail as if she has hurried, two more rings are in her ear, at the top. One is in the center of her ear, right through that flappy, soft part.

"Can you talk? You're Daniel, right?"

I nod. She's leaning forward, resting her thin body on the handle of her bicycle. It's an old bicycle, it looks very used and doesn't even have a bell or any lights as far as I can see. Her right pants leg is rolled up tightly and I see her calf and her knee. It's a very pretty knee.

"This is awkward", she says. "I thought you could speak. Denton didn't tell me you were a mute. To make things easier, nod again to signal me you're a retard. Don't nod to signal me you're having a stroke."

"Uh, yea. Hello", I manage. I try to think of a clever retort but fail. Caty turns around, as if to break the fourth wall with an invisible audience.

"It's alive", she says, astounded, to the invisible audience.

"Wow", I say.

"You like me?", she says.

"No, I mean yes, I do. I said 'wow' because you're really a bitch. Not just on the Internet."

"Yea, well, you'll get used to my sight. The first few nights you'll feel the desparate need to jerk off. Now I don't want you to feel alarmed. Everybody gets that. But eventually, seing me will be like second nature and you'll be able to form coherent sentences in my presence. Are you coming or what? There's too many fucking cops around here." She pushes her bicycle past me, hitting a bystander in the hip with the handle.

"Ey, watch where you're going, young lady!", says the guy.

"Fuck you, fatboy", she yells back, not even turning her head to look at him. I pick up my backpack and run after her.

"Bikes are forbidden in here", the guy screams after her.

***

"You want help with that?" I point to her bike, which she is half-pushing, half-carrying down the stairs towards the city.

"You couldn't handle it", she says. Her arm muscles work under her tan skin as she expertly guides the front wheel down the steps while elevating the back wheel just a few centimeters off the ground. I notice she has a bag over her shoulder. It bounces off the small of her back with each step she takes, making clap-clap sounds.

"One thing you have to learn, young Daniel, is that it's all in the details. They train you to obey the little things so you'll obey the big things later."

I stop as she pushes her bicycle into ongoing traffic on a red light and I curse.

"You're crazy!", I yell at her, on the other side of the street.

"You're losing me!", she yells back, laughing. Then she swings one shapely leg over her saddle. Fuck. I try to judge the speed of the oncoming cars, zig-zagging my way through them, every single one of them honking. As I arrive on the other side, she's standing in her pedals, balancing the bicycle in standstill. As if bored, she does a little bunny hop with the bike. Her pony tail whips around. She lifts the handle, bucks her hip and turns the bike almost on the spot. Then she turns to me, as if to make sure I'm still there. The pony tail follows sharply, whipping away from her neck. I can see something small and shiny there, another piercing. The orange streetlight reflects dimly in two silver spots before her pony tail comes back to rest and blocks my view. I wonder if she has any piercings in other places. Like her nipples.

"Let's go, slow poke. We haven't got all day." She pedals slowly, almost in slow motion, turning the handle to counter-balance from time to time.

"So, these guys at the venue...", I start.

"Oh, they're morons. Don't worry, we're only going there to make fun of them", says Caty.

"But it says on the event page that-"

"Yea, yea, you know these people. 'If only WE were elected'", she says, mocking a deep male voice, "'everything would be cool! If you vote for US, food will fall from the sky and babies will laugh all day.'"

I don't really know what to say to that, so I don't say anything.

"That was what I call an impression", she says, "it's this great idea I had. I said to myself: Hey, what if I pretended to be someone else and imitate their voice? I think it's going to be big."

"I think-"

"Oh, you already know about that? Let me tell you about this other thing I've invented. I call it 'irony', which is ironic, as I thought of it while ironing my panties."

I'm pretty sure she's mentally insane. Is this even the right girl? I haven't seen a picture of her. Maybe I just followed some random crazy chick into the Berlin night and Caty is still waiting for me at the station? I ponder the idea seriously for a moment. Then the faint clap-clap of her bag banging up against her hip calls me back. She is pretty hot. I'll just follow her some more.

".. and this guy is right on the way, so we'll just check by and I'll do my thing. You might learn something."

She's talking about some business of hers. I'm not sure I want to know, but hey, where else am I going to go?

***

The guy is a hulk. Easily two meters tall and built like a brick wall. I stay back slightly, as I don't know what to do. Against his massive frame, her thin body looks like a twig. She doesn't seem to mind though as she pulls some things from her bag and takes some money from the hulk. They mumble some more and the hulk looks around suspiciously, then takes off into an alley.

"Wow, that guy was massive", I say.

"Don't tell him or he'll get angry", she says, counting her money and putting it into her shoulder bag.

"What did you sell him?", I ask, trying to peek into her bag.

"Money", then she adds, "you wouldn't like him when he's angry."

"You sold him money?"

"Real money."

"Gold?"

"Silver. Too bad you guessed wrong, you could've kissed me."

I close my eyes and try to stop my mind from racing. She's just messing with me again. I shake my head out and she gets back on her bicycle.

"So", I ask, "is this place close? With the minarchists, I mean?"

She nods her head forward, chin and nose rising in unison, pony tail whipping. I squint my eyes and at the end of the street, I see some official looking people standing in front of a restaurant.

***

The restaurant is actually a restaurant slash bar slash hip place. It's packed. Damn these minarchists, but they know how to fill a place. There's posters and flyers and snacks.

"They have a projector", I whisper to Caty.

"You can't take your bike inside", says the man in the suit to Caty.

"I'm not leaving it out here so you can steal it", Caty says.

"I don't want your piece of shit", says the man.

"Is that what your father said when he saw you and left your mum?", says Caty.

I sigh.

"Just put it out back", says the man and spits accurately, missing Caty's sneakers only by centimeters.

***

"Aren't you going to lock it?", I ask when she just leans the bike against a wall and walks.

"Why? Who's going to steal it? Besides, nobody can handle it besides me."

"It's a bike, what's to handle?"

"Stop whining, it won't get you into my pants. And check out these", she says, grabbing a handful of mixed nuts from a table outside the restaurant. She throws her head back, pours them into her mouth and chews noisily.

I haven't eaten since I got on the train, but I'm nervous and not hungry. Caty is totally at ease or pretending to be, but I haven't been to many political conventions. There's quite a crowd inside the restaurant, most of them suited up and elegant. We're here in t-shirts and jeans and Caty hasn't even rolled down her right pant leg.

Caty pushes the glass door open and I am drowned in the noise of hundreds of talking voices. Someone's doing checks on the microphone. A few heads turn when we enter, but nobody seems to be interested in us much.

"HEY", Caty screams in my ear. I turn to hear her better.

"WHAT?", I scream back.

"I'M GOING TO DO SOME COKE IN THE BATHROOM, YOU WANNA COME?"

I'm certain somebody must've heard that, but nobody reacts.

"UH, NO, I'M GOOD. YOU GO AHEAD AND I'LL PICK US SEATS", I scream.

"OK. YOU SURE YOU DON'T WANT ANY COCAINE?", she screams. I give her the finger and she laughs. I can't hear her laugh, of course, it's too loud. But the wrinkles around her lips and the flashing teeth make her look even prettier.

***

I see some space on a bench towards the back of the room. The viewing angle to the projector isn't too great, you have to turn almost 90 degrees to see whoever's talking. I sit down and my neighbour smiles at me.

"Good to see friends of freedom", he says.

"Yes. Quite a turnout tonight, no?", I say.

"It's quite an event. You know, even HE will be here."

"Who?"

"You know, Bernd."

"I'm sorry, who's Bernd?"

The guy looks at me like I'm from mars. He's chubby and unshaven in a programmer sort of way. He wears a dress shirt that seems like an office uniform on him.

"Bernd Bach? Haven't you read his book?"

"No, I haven't. What's it about?"

"It's called The Socialist Conspiracy."

"Is it about socialism?"

"Not really, it's more about the conspiracy of the ruling and economic elites, how they make all the important decisions and stuff."

"I see", I lie.

"You should really read it. I came just to see him speak. He's a great speaker."

"Ok", I say, not really knowing what to reply. Caty, where are you?

"Are you in the truth movement?", he asks.

"Um, I'm not sure what you mean. I like truth, yes. I mean, who wants to be lied to, right?"

"No, I mean the Truth Movement, do you know about that?"

"I don't think so."

"Well, it's basically the movement demanding clarification and investigation of the September 11th attacks on the World Trade Center."

"Seriously?", I say.

"Of course! This event is the most important sign that the global power elites are plotting to take away our rights and freedoms to install a world-wide system of socialism!"

"Well", I say, "I agree socialism is bad. I don't want socialism."

"Exactly!", says my neighbour, then, "You should join the movement."

"I'll think about it", I say.

"Think about what? Me?", Caty says and I jerk my head to the left in surprise.

"Oh hey, there you are. How'd it go?"

"Yea, I'm about as high as a fucking kite. Can I sit down next to you?"
She's been staring at me intensely for 30 seconds without twitching or
blinking her eyes. That freaks me out.

"Sure", I say and slide closer to the truth guy. Caty turns around in a very
deliberate way and carefully sits her tiny ass down on the bench next to
me. Then she looks at me again, no expression on her face.

"I feel great. I'm glad you came", she says.

She turns her head very slowly to the podium.

"Thanks", I say, "but it's probably just the drugs."

Truth guy leans over.

"You shouldn't do drugs. The global power elites use them to control our
minds and distract us from the truth."

Caty keeps looking at the podium.

"I think I forgot my tinfoil hat", she says very loudly. Truth guy leans back
and refrains from further communication with us.

Minarchists
============

"Welcome to the convention of the Party of Rational Notions", says the
first speaker. He's very tall, like two meters tall for sure. He's also wearing
a suit. It makes him look like a thug.

"Lovers of liberty, friends of freedom. You've gathered here with us
tonight, because you feel angered. You feel betrayed. The government is
spending millions on entitlement programs and pet projects, ignoring the
real issues. Our tax money is wasted."

Applause. I applaud, too.

After some propaganda about the Party of Rational Notions, he introduces the first speaker. He's a law professor. He drones for what seems like hours about some parts of national and international law. Caty sits extremely still the whole time. Her back is perfectly straight and she never seems to move a muscle. I sneak in a few glances under the table, where her pant leg is still rolled up and her leg and knee are bare.

After the law professor, there's a break. I nudge Caty's shoulder and she turns to me. Her eyes are like brown flood lights. I don't know if it's the cocaine. Has she even done cocaine? Maybe she's just made fun of me again. Shouldn't she be extremely twitchy after doing cocaine?

"You wanna grab some nuts?", she says to me.

"Do you?", I retort cleverly.

"Sure, not your's though", she says and gets up. As she walks, she slowly loses the stiffness and her movements become more fluid and bouncy again. I suspect she's a robot. Trailing her and discreetly admiring her bare leg, I follow her to one of the bars. She grabs a bowl of mixed nuts and hogs it all for herself, shielding it with her forearms from the members of the Rational Party.

"So", says some random dude in a suit to her, "what did you think of the speech?"

Caty ignores him.

"Hey", he says, "I'm talking to you!" He waves his hand in front of her face.

Caty turns to him, smiles and points to her ears, shaking her head. Then she points to me.

"Oh", says Random Dude, "I'm sorry. I didn't realize your condition." To me: "Are you her translator?"

"Indeed", I say, "that's what I am."

"Tell her I ask her what she thought about the speech. I'm interested in her opinion."

I'm not sure if the guy's trying to hit on her, even though she plays deaf and mute. I nudge her shoulder, then give her some made-up sign language with my hands. I sign her timeout, goggles, going to sleep and money. She replies goggles, two, walking and blowjob. Blowjob looks pretty explicit and Random Guy makes big eyes.

"She says she appreciates your asking", I invent, "and she especially liked the professor's mentioning of the irony of the definition of taxation as non-theft being given by the perpetrator, i.e. the state, itself."

Random Guy nods in agreement.

"Tell her that I think its great for a young lady, such as herself, to involve herself in politics."

I sign her four, kiss, beating heart and striking a match. She replies writing, playing the violin, snorting cocaine and stirring in a pot.

"She says she hates politics, she can't stand it."

"But then why is she attending a congress of the Party of Rational Notions?", Random Guy wonders out loud. I now see the Party badge on his suit. Caty puts handfuls of mixed nuts in her mouth at a time, happily crunching and chewing in his direction, as if to be disrespectful on purpose. She even starts dribbling pieces of chewed-up nuts on the bar table. I wonder if she's playing retarded too. I sign her eating with a spoon, cutting a pizza, riding the bicycle and money. I'm starting to run out of made up signs. How many signs do mutes actually have? I have no idea. Maybe they only have like thirty signs? The alphabet only has 26 characters. Caty replies with picking her nose, brushing her teeth, wiping her ass and riding the bicycle. She likes my riding the bicycle sign. I smile. She smiles back, then continues chewing.

"Uh, there's several reasons. One is general interest, to check you guys out. Check out your politics, I mean. Not check you personally out. There's also the profound desire to socialize with other liberty-minded individuals on her part. Libertarianism isn't very big in the mute community."

"I thought she was deaf?"

"Both. Mute and deaf. She can technically make sounds, but the second she opens her mouth, only garbage comes out. It isn't pretty to hear. She'd rather not scare you with what she considers a 'foul mouth'."

"Did she just say that?"

I peek over to see Caty pour the entire remaining contents of the mixed nuts bowl into her lips.

"No, that's just what she'd say. We get asked this question a lot, so I just pulled it from the cache."

"Cache?"

"It's a computer term."

"Uh-hu", says Random Guys, "So, what is she doing later?"

I can't believe it. He's hitting on a deaf and mute girl who's here with her interpreter. Then again, wouldn't mute and deaf girls like to be hit on? I can't imagine why they wouldn't. It's probably very lonely to be deaf and mute and have nobody hit on you. I sign Caty looking at my watch, sleepy, blowjob and walking. She replies bicycle, money, hand job (her mouth is still too full to sign blowjob) and hanging herself. Random Dude looks scared by the hanging sign, so I try to calm him down.

"Don't worry. She says she's gonna ride her bicycle, make some money, give me a hand job and then go to sleep."

"Hanging is the sign for go to sleep?"

"Yea, it's like, the dead are only sleeping, you know?"

"But you signed her this earlier", he makes the sleepy sign, "what does that mean?"

"That's 'tonight'." Caty, still chewing, nudges me. She signs hand job again and points to Random Guy.

"She says she can give you a hand job too, if you want to come. We're in a hotel close by."

Random Guy blushes and looks around if someone heard what I said. Caty signs long, kiss, hand job, looking at watch.

"She says she's gonna love you long time", I say. I don't find out if Random Dude gets my inside joke as Caty chokes, coughs, spits a large mouthful of chewed up mixed nuts all over his face and his suit and the table, and collapses laughing into the bar table, still coughing pieces of nuts and raisins everywhere. Random Dude is not amused and storms off. I try to steady Caty and clap her on the back as hard as I can, to get the nuts in her wind pipe loose. She shoots some more over the bar, her face all red and her eyes almost in tears from laughing and coughing. I want to clap her back again, but she pushes my hand away.

"Dude", she says, "that guy's PISSED."

She smiles. I smile back.

"Maybe we should leave", I say.

"Fuck no", she says, "I have lots of nuts to chew."

We take seats in another part of the room, where neither Dirty Programmer Tinfoil Hat Man nor Random Mixed Nut Suit Man are close. The thuggish Party Leader appears again and announces the main speaker of the evening, Bernd Bach himself. Bach is kind of bald, but you can't really hold that against him. He tells how he lost his job for telling the truth about finance and the money conspiracy and I sympathize. He makes himself out as a fighter against the evils of central banking and legal tender laws. I applaud. His speech is a little confused and he doesn't know his PowerPoint slides very well. He says he's a global warming skeptic and some other things. I'm not blown away by his speech, but not as bored as I was by the law professor's.

He gets lots of applause. I can tell these people love him, and he's a fun speaker. He gets the emotions rolling. He's answering questions after the talk when some crazy woman gets up and starts yelling.

"You people all know it! We can't pretend it's not true!", she says broadly, probably to everyone. Bernd Bach looks annoyed.

"What are you talking about?"

"I'm talking about the Corporate Republic of Germany!", she says, "Our country is run as a massive corporation, it's even in the law! And there's still US army bases everywhere! They've made us their employees, we work for their wars!"

Bernd Bach doesn't want to talk to this woman. He tells her to sit down and please, everybody, only ask questions related to the talk.

Afterwards we see him outside, smoking a cigarette. Caty goes outside and I follow her and her shapely legs. She just walks up to Bach and asks him for a cigarette. He fumbles in his pockets.

"You smoke?", I ask Caty.

"No", she says, "Not usually anymore. I quit."

Bach hesitates.

"Then maybe I shouldn't be giving you a smoke", he says.

"Maybe", Caty says in what seems to me like a moment of rare clarity. Bach puts his cigarette pack away and continues blowing smoke rings.

"Are you members? Of the Party of Rational Notions, I mean?", he says. I shake my head.

"We don't believe in the circus", Caty says.

"Circus?", Bach asks.

"Politics", Caty says.

"What do the young people today believe in, if you don't mind me asking?"

"Direct Action", Caty says. Bach eyes her suspiciously.

"You guys are anarchists? You want to throw bombs?"

"Yes and no", Caty says, "our direct action is trade." She opens her book bag and lets him peek inside. I lean forward and want to take a peek too, but I can't see. She shakes the bag a bit and I hear the metallic rattle of coins or something. Bach makes big eyes.

"Build new institutions in the shell of the dying state", I offer.

"Carson?", Caty says

"But without a state", Bach says, pointing his cigarette at Caty, "who would build the roads?" Caty gives him a pat on the shoulder.

"One day, man, one day", she says. Then she turns and goes back inside. Her book bag clangs against her back with each step, luring me to follow her. Bach shakes his head and is probably already forgetting about us. Minarchists usually do.

***

The last speaker is a younger guy, maybe 25 or 28. He seems a bit nervous, probably not an experienced public speaker. He's also wearing a suit. He's talking about Austrian Economics and how people are slowly waking up to the truth. These people love the truth. He says inflation can't go on much further without serious financial impact. He says people are realizing the financial crisis has not been caused by greedy capitalists but by monetary policy and regulations.

After the talk, nobody asks him questions, so I get up and walk to the microphone.

"That was a good talk, and I really love Austrian Economics", I say. He smiles and thanks me.

"But Austrian Economics has been around how long? Boehm-Bawerk, 1880s? Mises wrote Human Action in the 1930s or 40s, right?"

He nods and asks what my point is.

"My point is: The truth has been out there for about 70-120 years. Why should everyone start believing it now?"

"The Internet", he says, "and the financial crisis." I think for a second.

"I hope you're right", I say. "I don't believe playing politics is going to do any good, but man, I sure hope you're right. Good luck."

***

Caty gets her bicycle from the back alley and we walk back the way we came. She's pushing the bicycle and from time to time, the pedal hits her in the calf. She doesn't even seem to notice.

"That was good, in the end", she says, "classy."

"Thanks."

"How much do you know about Austrian Economics?"

"I've read Human Action", I say.

"How'd you like it?"

"I think it's amazing. Mises was a bright guy."

"Not an anarchist, though", she says.

"He'd be an anarchist today, I'm sure of it", I say, "back in the day, he was the only one even daring to oppose socialism. Anything less than total socialism was complete liberty for him, I guess. If he could see and live in a modern democracy, he'd surely be an anarcho-capitalist."

"You're probably right", she says.

"What's with you, you're so mellow. Did the talks make you tired?"

"I just don't feel like bitching right now. Come on, let's meet the others."

Denton
======

Caty puts her bicycle against the wall. We're standing in front of what seems like a hipster cocktail bar. There's a big neon sign saying "Capitalism is Murder". Caty pushes the door open. Blaring loud music. I follow her inside. We go down a flight of stairs and there's another door. A security guy is standing there with his arms crossed in front of his chest, busy looking real buff. Caty says something, points to me, and the guy opens the door for us. I nod to him and he nods back. Still looks grim though.

The music is even louder inside. The cocktail bar is built into some kind of cellar or dungeon. There's bare stone walls and arches. Nothing is symmetric. The walls seem to cave in under the building sitting atop of them. Hip people in their late twenties sit on tiny bar stools and drink large cocktails with straws. The music is some weird mixture of electronics and jungle noise. Sounds like an aztec drummer fell into a digital recording studio. There's pan flutes.

Caty strolls slowly through the room, heading towards the back. Some of the hip guys look at her as she sways by. In the dim dungeon lighting, it seems as if she's floating. I can now see a heavy curtain in the back. Probably some kind of VIP room. Caty stops in front of the curtain and turns around, facing me. I'm about to pull the curtain aside, but she grabs my wrist and stops me. Putting her finger to her lips, she signs me to be still. Then she sticks her hand inside her book bag. She pulls out a tiny plastic bag filled with white powder. She extends her hand towards me, offering me some. The bag lies in her palm, her long fingers closing slowly above it as I decline her offer. She snaps the rubber band from the bag expertly with the fingers of her other hand, licks her index finger and stubs it inside the bag. A few of the tiny white crystals stick to her finger tip and she continues rubbing them between her upper lip and her front teeth. She blinks and rubs her tongue against her teeth. I can only now see that she has a piercing in the middle of her tongue, blinking in the dark recess of her mouth like hidden treasure. She pulls me closer and her lips are near my ear. I can feel her breathing.

"No turn unstoned", she whispers, barely audible in between the psychedelic jungle beats. Then she pushes me away from her and turns towards the curtain. With a grandiose gesture, she pulls it open. I feel her hand on my back as she motions for me to go in.

If the main floor of the bar is a dungeon, this is a sultan's cave. The walls are covered in purple carpets. There's a low table, around which four people sit, or rather lie, as there's no chairs, only oriental chair cushions. The guy furthest away from me is smoking a water pipe that sits on the table before him. The one closest to me turns around slowly, facing me. He's wearing a white robe with large, drooping arms. His dark brown hair falls far below his shoulders, almost touching the chair cushion he's sitting on. He smiles and motions with his robed arm for me to sit down on another chair cushion. I feel Caty's hand in my back, pushing me forward.

"You must be Denton", I say to the robed guy. He nods slowly. I take off my jacket, and, not knowing where to put it, throw it on the floor behind my chair cushion. Then I sit down. The cushion is soft and I'm literally laid back. I look around, but there's no hurry. Nobody's saying anything for a while. I look back up at Caty. She's standing between Denton and me, her arms crossed in front of her chest, and for the first time I notice how slender she really is.

"Look what the cat dragged in", the guy to my right finally says.

"Fuck you, Michael", Caty says.

"Hi, I'm Michael", says the guy to me and shakes my hand. He's the most generic looking person I've ever seen. He looks so normal I've almost forgotten his face, even though I'm still looking at it. He's not really tall, but not small either. I wouldn't describe him as pudgy, but he isn't cut. His hair is a very nondescript brown-blonde and his voice could put him anywhere from 16 to 45.

"Hello, I'm Daniel", I say.

"I know. Wax on, wax off."

"What?"

"Forget it."

I turn to Denton and offer him my hand. He makes a gesture of shaking it. After we shake hands, he returns into a kind of praying position with his hands folded together in the robe in front of him. I lean forward and shake the hands of the other guys. One's called Paul and one introduces himself as Faust, though I doubt that's his real name. Faust wears a tie.

There's another empty cushion at the far end, next to Faust, who's still smoking the water pipe. I expect Caty to sit down over there, but she pushes Denton to the side a little on his cushion, forcing her tiny ass down besides him. She puts her head on his shoulder and her eyes stare into the distance as if she's dreaming.

"What are you doing?", Denton says.

"Touching you", Caty says.

"You know the deal, Caty."

"I don't like the deal."

"And I don't like to make out with coked-up bitches. Get off the cocaine or get off of me."

Caty sighs and gets up. She walks over to Faust and plops down on the empty cushion. They fist-bump. Faust doesn't stop smoking his water pipe for a second. There's a few bottles on the table, I now realize, as Caty pours herself a drink.

"So Daniel", Denton says, "Caty tells me you're into agorism?"

"Well", I say, "'into agorism' is a bit much. I think it's interesting. I haven't actually done anything."

"Let me put it this way", he says, "do you believe in aggression?"

"No", I say.

"Do you believe in organized aggression?"

"No."

"Do you want to support organized aggression?"

"No."

"Then why are you paying taxes?"

"I'm not paying taxes, I'm a student."

"Hypothetically."

"Uh, I guess I shouldn't be paying taxes. I would be supporting organized aggression, right?"

"Very good, Daniel. You are into agorism, you just don't know it yet."

He seems satisfied. I look around, but there doesn't seem to exist a need for further communication. They're all content just sitting around and enjoying themselves. After a few seconds of silence, Faust hands his water pipe to Caty.

"Daniel isn't your real name, is it?", he says.

"Yes, it is."

"Dude, never use your real name", he says.

"Why not?"

"Let's just say", Michael interrupts, "hypothetically, of course, that one of us gets caught by the cops, riding her bicycle across a red light, high as a fucking kite, with a bag full of drugs and precious metals."

Caty leans over and blows smoke from the water pipe into his face. He turns around, gives her a "Seriously?" look, then turns back to me.

"Let's further assume that this person knows your real name or your address or anything. Do you think the cops can beat your name out of a 23 year old girl?"

I look at Caty and she rolls her eyes. I'm not sure if that's a good sign.

"They could, probably."

"Exactly. They most probably could. That's what they live for, scaring the shit out of innocent people. So I'd advise you to come up with some pseudonym."

"Well put, Michael", says Denton.

"I don't know why you guys keep this faggot around", Caty says, pointing to Michael.

"Not everyone's a faggot just because they don't want to touch you, even with gloves on", Michael says.

"Are you saying you don't want this?" She puts a hand down the front of her jeans.

"I'm saying I don't want your cooties."

"My cooties never hurt anyone, you know", she says, hand still in pants. I wonder about the presence of piercings down there.

"Be quiet, kids", Denton says. He reaches his hand into a pocket, hidden somewhere in his robe, and returns it holding a very used book. He puts it on the table in front of me and pushes it closer. It's called "Alongside Night" by one J. Neil Schulman.

"Take this and read it", he says, nodding towards me. I take the book and thumb through it. About 200 pages. I put it next to my jacket on the floor so I don't forget it. I get to do a lot of reading lately.

Looking over to Caty, I see her fumbling with another bottle. I'm trying to think of something to say, but can't come up with anything.

"Don't worry", says Denton, "just have a good time."

We sit around for a while. Faust smokes his water pipe. Caty drinks at least four glasses of some liquor. Denton seems to either pray or meditate. Or maybe he's fallen asleep with his eyes open.

"So", says Michael, "I'm going to get us some girls."

"Sure", Faust manages between hits from his pipe, "girls are nice." I look at Denton, but he doesn't really seem to be focused on any girls. Much to the dismay of Caty. She's eyeing him from her chair cushion. She's playing with a glass of liquor in her fingers, swirling it clockwise and then counterclockwise, ice cubes clacking against each other.

Michael gets up and vanishes through the curtain. I'm not sure, but I could swear he didn't even pull the curtain aside. He just went - through.

"So Paul", I start, "What kind of stuff do you do?"

"Oh, you know...", he says.

"I don't, that's why I'm asking", I say.

"If you must, I do some ForEx and some OTC."

"OTC?"

"Over the counter. I trade digital money for physical money."

"So if I give you BitCoins you give me Euros?"

"Yes."

I nod. Then I ask:

"What do you do with all the BitCoins, though?"

"Sell them."

"To whom?"

"People who want BitCoins."

I nod again. The curtain moves and I look up. I hear some giggling. Then a very female hand pierces through and the curtain is pulled aside. It's Michael with two girls. Maybe sisters. Or good friends. They have some kind of partner look going on. Both very blonde, very high heels, very short skirt, very deep cleavage. They're almost bursting with excitement. Michael has one hand around each of the girls' hips.

"That over there is Faust", Michael says, pointing a finger. He nudges the smaller girl and she scurries over.

"This is the new guy", Michael says, pointing to me. He releases the tall girl's hip, but she's not moving.

"Who's he? In the robe?", she whispers loudly.

"Oh him, that's Denton", says Michael.

The tall girl hesitantly walks over to Denton, who's not reacting to her presence at all. Her steps are silent on the thick carpet, but I feel the vibrations in the floor. She stops between Denton and me, facing him, and bends over. Her cleavage is almost directly in front of his face. She wipes a strand of hair out of her face. From the low position of the chair cushion, I get a nice view of her ass in the short skirt. I consider sliding down in my seat to peek up her skirt, but that's probably too creepy.

"Hello", she says, all smiles.

"Hi there", Denton says, looking up, "what's your name?"

"Julia", the tall girl says. She's still standing bent over. If she'd open her hips now, she'd grind her vagina into Denton's face. He seems unphazed.

"I'm Denton", Denton says, "Pleasure to meet you, Julia."

I take a glance to the right and Caty's looking semi-frustrated. Her glass is empty. She's leaning back and has got her feet propped up under her ass cheeks on the cushion chair, knees high in the air and spread. She's looking in our direction from between her thighs. I can't really tell if she's angry at Michael for bringing girls. I try to smile at her, but it comes out wrong. She looks at me weakly, not really interested.

***

Michael has reclaimed his seat between Caty and me. He leans over.

"Sorry, man. She was supposed to be yours."

"I'm good", I say, "thanks though."

Julia seems fascinated by Denton and keeps asking him questions. They've moved from his robe to religion to spirituality. Denton believes in some stuff I've never heard of. He's probably made it up himself. Marie, as the smaller girl is called, is making out with Faust over at the water pipe.

"Hey Michael", I say, "what'd you say to get them here?"

"It's not about what you say", Michael says.

"What did you DO, then?"

"I asked them to come."

"Huh", I say. I think.

"But then it was about what you said, wasn't it?", I ask.

"No. The words didn't matter. What mattered was that I asked them to come with me."

"I don't get it."

"The very act of asking the girls to come with me was what mattered. They didn't care what words I used or how I phrased it."

"You're pretty good at this", I say.

"Practice", Michael says.

"Hey Caty", I say, leaning over the table, "too bad Michael didn't bring a girl for you, huh?"

"Too bad", she says.

"You want me to get you a girl?", Michael offers.

"Nah, I'm good. I'll just watch this one", Caty says, pointing her finger at Julia. I'm about to say something, but Caty hushes me and points to Julia again.

"What? Why not?", Julia says, almost insulted.

"I'm sorry", Denton says, "it's not that you're not hot. I'm married."

"Fuck married", Julia says, "what does your wife care if you fuck me?"

"She wouldn't", says Denton, "I do."

"Fuck you", Julia says and gets up.

"It's been nice talking to you", Denton says very serenely.

"Shut up, freak. Marie, are you coming?" She straightens her top and gathers her purse. Marie seems too involved with Faust to respond. Her tongue is in his throat and I can't see where his left hand is. Wherever, she seems to be enjoying it.

"So Julia", I begin, "how would you like to make out with Caty over there?"

"Creep", Julia says.

"She's been eyeing you all night", I say. Caty nods enthusiastically.

"It's true", she says, "I think we might be soul mates."

"There's something wrong with you two", Michael says more to himself.

"I don't do skinny bitches", Julia says.

"Too bad", Caty says, making a sad-smiley mouth, "we could've done this! It's great fun!" She makes an O with the index finger and thumb of her left hand, then slowly forces through the fingers of her right. Julia stares. Caty manages to force her knuckles through the tight ring and it suddenly dawns on me that she's imitating putting her fist into Julia's cunt.

"You people are all freaks", Julia says.

"Observe", Caty says. Her finger-O is now encircling her thin wrist. Suddenly, she snaps open her fist like a sprung trap, stretching her fingers out in all directions. Julia winces, then gathers herself.

"Marie!", she almost yells, "are you coming?!" Marie is torn between making out with Faust and following her friend/sister's yelling. Too bad when you're not the alpha girl, I guess. She gives Faust one last big kiss, picks up her purse and runs towards Julia.

"Call me", Marie whispers loudly to Faust.

"Yeah right", Faust says. Julia storms through the curtain, pulling Marie with her. The curtain swings a little and comes to a halt.

"Wow", Caty says, "you and the ladies, Michael. I'm impressed." Michael sighs.

"I wouldn't have gotten her if I'd known she'd obsess about Denton."

"Maybe you shouldn't have gotten nymphos again", Denton says.

"She wasn't supposed to be into you. New guy likes nymphos", Michael says.

"I appreciate the effort", I say.

Caty pours herself another drink.

10 Euros per night
========================

Caty's pretty much unconscious. Her left arm is around my shoulder, her right arm around Denton's shoulder, and we drag slash carry her out of the bar. Outside, Michael, Faust and Paul are waiting in front of a 5 Series BMW, engine running.

"She's so shitfaced", Faust says and smiles.

"Yea, she might have a little substance abuse problem", I say.

"Or three", Michael says. Paul doesn't say anything, he just looks at his watch.

"I have to hurry, can you bring her home?", he says.

"Not home, but she can stay in the notel with new guy", Denton says. He turns to me.

"Promise me you won't rape her", he says.

"Do I look like a rapist?", I say, a little outraged.

"They never do."

"Whatever. I promise. What's a notel?"

"It's not a hotel", Michael hints, "and it's where you're sleeping."

Paul gets into the drivers seat and Michael and Faust get in too. They speed off. Denton shifts a little, moving Caty's weight on his back. I grab her arm to not let her fall.

"What about her bike?", I say.

"She can get it tomorrow. I'm not her babysitter." He shoulders his half of Caty's weight and starts walking. He's stronger than he looks.

We drag slash carry her for only about 5 minutes, when Denton stops in front of some residential looking house. He pulls out a cell phone and types a few things. After fuzzing with it for about a minute, the doors make a quiet clicking sound. He puts the phone away and pushes the door open. I put my arm under Caty's knees and carry her fairytale-style up the stairs. Too bad she can't see me right now.

"What's with the phone?", I say, "That was impressive."

"I booked the notel room", Denton says.

"With your phone?" I pant a little. Thank fuck she's so light! I don't think I could've carried Julia up the stairs.

"It's a website. You make an online transaction and you get the room."

"What about the remote door?"

"What do you expect, a doorman? Do you know how many embedded servers I can link to an electronic lock for even a month worth of paying a single person?"

We've arrived at the top of the stairs and Denton leads me to the end of a corridor. There's no numbers on the door or anything like a hotel would have. Caty's feet drag on the floor as I shove her through the door. There's a two person bed inside and I plop her down onto the mattress. Denton checks some things in the room. He seems very methodical.

"Okay", he says, "there's everything you need. Toothbrush, paste, soap, towels. Don't worry about the reservation. We'll talk tomorrow."

"Thanks", I says.

"Don't worry. It's only 10 Euros."

"10 Euros? For this room?"

"Sure. 10 Euros times 10 residents times 30 days equals 3000 Euros a month. There's no restaurant and no hotel bar, though."

"Huh", I say, then: "You think I should wake her or undress her or put a blanket over her or something?"

"Yea, a blanket's probably a good idea. We wouldn't want her to get a cold."

I crawl on the bed to pull Caty closer towards the cushion. I manage to pull her head somewhat in the vicinity of the cushion and stop. I don't know if she's dreaming, but she slowly curls up into an embryo figure and hugs the cushion.

"Her pant leg is still rolled up", I say. Denton smiles. Caty purrs in her dream.

"Too bad she's such a junkie. She's beautiful", Denton says.

"You like her? She was totally into you. She was looking at you and that girl all night."

Denton sighs.

"Daniel, there's around a billion hot girls on the planet. I'm not sleeping with any one of them besides my wife."

"Because of your religion?"

"No, because I choose not to."

"Why do you choose not to?", I say.

"She's my wife and I like that", he says. He pulls a blanket over Caty and she snuggles into it in her sleep.

"Why is she doing cocaine all the time?", I ask Denton.

"I don't know", Denton says, "but I worry, too."

"I think I love her", I say.

"That's your problem. Just remember what drugs can do to people."

"What do you mean?", I say.

"Ask her to look you in the eyes and tell you she didn't do any coke today", Denton says.

On his way out, he points to a laptop sitting on the desk.

"There's a WhisperPC prototype. If you want to surf the net or check your email, feel free."

"Ok", I say, "see you tomorrow. Tell your wife I said 'hi'."

"I will", Denton says, "good night."

AgoristCookbook.com
=====================

I wake up to slight snoring. Sunlight is coming through the window, casting the room in bright white. I yawn and sit back against the cushion. Caty has snuggled up against me under her blanket. She's invaded my half of the double bed with her head, one arm and one leg. I try to move out under the blanket and out of the bed without waking her. I fail.

"Don't leave", she purrs. Her voice is sleepy and hoarse.

"I'm not going to leave", I say.

"I mean don't leave the bed", she says, eyes still closed. She reaches her hand over, grasping my arm and pulling me closer. Her fingers are hot on my skin. She snuggles closer. Our blankets are now a tangled mass. I lie still and enjoy the warmth radiating off her body, heating up the space under the blankets like an oven. Her eyes are still closed, long lashes contrasting on her skin. Her hair's bunched up between her head and the cushion, all black, all matte. I observe the ring in the wing of her nose rise and fall with each breath she takes. Her nostrils flare open and sink in on themselves as her lungs pump oxygen into her body. She pulls my arm close and leglocks me with her thighs. I'm lying still on my back and she's curled up against me as if to dryhump me. We're both fully clothed, I realize, but it still feels pretty intimate. I like it.

***

Later she's in the shower. I hear the water splash onto her naked body and open the laptop Denton left, to distract myself from the thought.
At the login it prompts me for some account credentials that Denton has written on a post-it note.

Account-ID: 555-738-983
Password: ********

I check mtgox.com and find BitCoin has passed the US Dollar. It is now hovering around $1.1.

I surf around and Twitter a little. There's some interview with Peter Schiff, but the laptop doesn't have Flash installed. Some kind of crypto-tricked-out Arch Linux, it seems. I answer in the boards and then check my email.

From: Tom Taylor <tom_ancap@mailvault.com>
To: Daniel LaRusso <daniel@mailvault.com>
Subject: check tihs out

dude check this out:
agoristcookbook.com

i'm trying to open a coding business. already got 1 client. woo! he's from singapore.
try it, its easy. you just code for people over the Internet and accept paypal on a fake name or bitcoin if they know what that is. should probably launder the money around a bit
before sending it to my real account.

I open a browser and type in the address. The splash site is a parody of the original Anarchist Cookbook. It says Anarchy - Agora - Action!

"What is Agorism?

Agorism, from the greek agora (marketplace), is the practice of completely voluntary exchange between two consenting parties. This can take many forms. Trade, services, restaurants, for profit, non profit, black market, white market, grey market. The only defining characteristics of agorist action is that it be completely voluntary, and thus outside the regulation or control of any government."

It goes on to explain that agorism is what everybody would be doing if there were no coercive government - just do what they would like to do, voluntary. There is black market activity, which the state forbids, like certain drugs or weapons. There's white market activity, where the activity itself isn't forbidden by the state, it's just being done without subjection to the state. This would include an agorist restaurant or bank. There's more variants, but I only skip over them.

Agorism seems to be the non-political strategy of achieving anarchism. Instead of voting at the booth every 4 years, hoping your idiot is going to win and keep his promises, agorism is taking matters into your own hands. Act as if the state didn't exist to make it disappear. Of course, the state is probably going to put you into prison if you start selling your defensive services under its nose. So you might have to be sneaky, at least in the beginning. The state doesn't like competition.

***

There's a noise from the bathroom. I realize the shower has stopped. I turn and Caty stands there, completely naked, semi-dry. I stare.

"What? Haven't you seen a naked girl before?", she says, smiling.

"I- um, well, not you", I manage. She looks confused.

"You haven't? Didn't we fuck last night?"

"No", I say.

"Oh", she says, "well, that explains the clothes. And my coochy's kinda dry. I was wondering."

"Yea."

"Did we at least make out?"

"No", I say.

"What are you, gay? Why didn't we make out?"

"I, um. You were drunk. Unconscious slash asleep."

"Why didn't we make out before I was unconscious slash asleep?"

"I don't know", I say. "We can still make out now, if you like", I add.

"Fuck that. I don't remember anything, but there was probably a damn good reason why I didn't make out with you."

I don't say anything to that. I try to not stare at her, but I fail miserably. I can't decide where to look. When she puts clothes on, I forget almost everything immediately. I try to cling to the mental image, but can only make out single parts of her body in my mind. The toned muscles of her stomach. The wide space between her thighs, with a glimpse of short black pubes. I think there was a piercing in her left nipple. The crease dissappearing beneath her ass cheek as she puts her leg into her pants.

She finishes by rolling up her right pants leg again, then looks at me.

"Is this going to be awkward or can we just eat some breakfast?", she says.

"Breakfast", I say.

***

I watch as Caty stuffs her mouth full of chocolate croissant. To say she eats like an ogress is unfair to ogres. One half of the croissant is still stuck in her throat while she forcefully presses on the other end, trying to cram it into her lips. Her throat convulses, carrying one third of the croissant, making room for more in her mouth. She manages to shovel the remaining bits in and close her lips. I'm curious how she plans to facilitate the transfer of the whole croissant from her mouth to her stomach. As if performing for a live audience, she raises her index finger in a "watch this" gesture. She grabs her extra large cup of exotic italian or french or aztec coffee in both hands. It's at least a quarter liter, probably closer to half a liter of steaming hot gourmet coffee. She brings the cup to her lips. I watch incredulous as she pours half a liter of hot, expensive, designer-, fashion-coffee down her throat, washing away the croissant that was stuck in there without a trace. She probably has no nerve endings left in her mouth or throat at all.

I catch myself staring again. She lets out a burp that sounds both wet and solid. Then she sighs and slides back in her leather-clad cafe armchair, patting her belly.

"Wow", I say and take a bite of my chocolate croissant, "you like to swallow."

"Careful", she says, "you could be next!"

I try to remember if I've seen her take drugs this morning. I can't really say, but then again she was in the bathroom for some time. I watch her nose as she talks, trying to identify suspicious twitching or sniffing. The silver ring dances as her lips move.

***

"So what do you do for fun? Besides riding your bicycle, I mean."

"You know, this and that", she says, "go out, dance, balance my books."

I chuckle.

"What?", she says.

"You balance your books for fun?"

"Yes", she says.

"Don't you think that's a little.. weird? For someone like you?"

"What, so I can't have fun doing accounting because I'm a girl? What are you, a racist?"

"I don't think that would technically be called a racist", I say.

"Stop patronizing me, you jerk!", she says to me. To the rest of the cafe she declares loudly:

"He's a misogynist. That's probably why I didn't fuck him last night."

My face turns a slight red. Luckily, nobody else is really interested in why Caty didn't fuck me last night.

"I'm serious", she adds, trying to make eye contact with some of the other guests, "he hates women."

When nobody listens, she shrugs her shoulders. Her attention turns back to me.

"Are you going to eat that?" She points at my half-eaten croissant.

"I plan to", I say, "why don't you drink another liter of boiling hot coffee?"

"I just might", she says, "I wasn't kidding, though."

"About what?"

"Accounting. I'm like a natural genius. It's a game for me."

"Isn't it just numbers?"

"It's not just any numbers. One column is your income. That's money you make. The other column is expenditures. That's money you lose. In some way, we all balance our income and expenditures, if only unconsciously. Accounting just makes a formal process out of it. Balancing books is the most vital skill there is. If you spend more than you earn, you die."

"You don't literally die", I say.

"Not today. Or with well meaning friends. But imagine you're a caveman or on a deserted island. If you eat 5 coconuts and only collect 3 new ones, you won't eat dinner the next day. Do that a few times and you starve. Accounting is really about life and death."

"Hm", I make, "I haven't really seen it like that before, I guess."

"That's typical of you. You don't know shit about my hobbies but you make fun of me. You're such an idiot. It's no wonder I didn't fuck you last night."

"I get it. You didn't fuck me. Can we please move on?"

She sighs.

"I'm just wondering why. I don't usually play hard to get. I'm always up for a bit of fun. Why wouldn't I fuck you?"

"You only had eyes for Denton and that blonde chick."

"I don't remember any blonde chick. Was she hot?"

"She was ok, I guess. You were getting pretty drunk."

"Then she was probably hot. What did you do?"

"Do? I didn't do anything."

"That's your problem, Daniel. If you don't make an offer, I can't take it."

"Why didn't you make an offer?"

"I obviously had better things to do", Caty says.

"Like getting thrashed?"

"Yes, like getting thrashed. And don't sound so condescending. I'm not the one who appeared less exciting than getting drunk."

"You were on drugs. And you were hitting on Denton."

"If your buyer is more interested in another offer, you have to surpass that offer or no deal. What is your strategy, waiting until someone takes your deal out of pity? How's that working out for you?"

"None of your business", I say. It feels more defensive than it should.

"Of course it's my business. As a prospective buyer, I'm very interested in past customers' experiences with your offer and services. There's no marketing as good as word of mouth."

"What about your "past customers"?"

"Not one of them has made use of my extremely generous return policy", Caty says.

"Can you please stop talking like it's some kind of economics thing?"

She hesitates. Her large brown eyes stare at me. I can see a flicker of uncertainty in her gaze.

"But it is like economics", she says.

"No it isn't", I say. I don't want to talk about relationships anymore.

"Wait, wait. Explain to me how this isn't exactly like economics."

"I'm not a seller. You're not a buyer. And I'm not telling you what my exes think about my 'services'."

"Ok", she says, "I hate to be the one to break this to you. But you're completely wrong."

"Not everything-", I try to say, but she cuts me off.

"This is a market process, Daniel. We're both individuals looking at the market to meet our needs. Your need is to fuck a girl you think is hot. My need is to get fucked by a guy I think is hot. I'd say we can agree that there is a baseline we can work with. You're obviously hot for me and I like you too. What needs to happen now is that we find a deal we both agree on. If we don't, we have to satisfy our needs elsewhere or leave them unsatisfied. Your move, Karate Kid!"

She has really talked herself into an economics-frenzy. I hate how she has just explained our current and potential sexual relationship using subjective value theory.

She sits there, leaning forward, waiting for me to say something. But I don't know what to say. After a few seconds, the fire in her eyes goes out and she leans back, grabbing her messenger bag.

"Listen", she says, "I've been ranting again. I should medicate myself a little to calm down."

"No", I say and put my arm forward to grab her wrist, "you're doing it wrong! Cocaine's supposed to get you high, not chill you out!"

She puts her bag down.

"And I like it when you rant", I say.

She smiles.

"That was pretty smooth", she says.

She stands up, puts her hands on the table, leaning over me, and gives me a kiss on the nose.

OpenTransactions
=================

```
*You have joined #agora
daniel: hi
shiz: moin
Bill: Hello
FellowTraveler: moin
daniel: shiz, ft: are you german??
shiz: no
daniel: why do you say moin
shiz: it means hi
daniel: i know what it means, but its a german slang. why do you say it?
*shiz shrugs
FellowTraveler: its just what agorists say
FellowTraveler: probably pirate slang
daniel: guess so
FellowTraveler: daniel: have you made any progress on your OT client?
daniel: sorry haven't done anything :( i know
FellowTraveler: too bad :(
FellowTraveler: there's another guy, though. he's done a lot using perl.
daniel: nice! does he have a running client?
FellowTraveler: yes, it's called the tempest client
FellowTraveler: https://github.com/dspearson/tempest
```

I check out the client. It's command line, but hey, it works. Mine doesn't work, so I can't really complain. I do some testing using the test-wallet that's included. Mint some money, send it to myself, send it to a test account, write a cheque, convert some of it into a quasi-banknote.

```
daniel: sweet, looks like he's got everything implemented
```

FellowTraveler: not everything, there's the new stuff. like baskets, automated selling, markets..
daniel: ok but i can send money
FellowTraveler: yes
daniel: that's the big part, right?
FellowTraveler: i guess
daniel: say, can you launder money with OT?
FellowTaveler: you could, but why would you? OT is completely 100% anonymous and untraceable.
daniel: oh. i have a friend who's going to love this when its ready
FellowTraveler: there's a spinoff project where one guy works on top of tempest to build a webclient
daniel: nice
FellowTraveler: yes. and i'm trying to find someone with android skills to make POS possible
daniel: piece of shit?
FellowTraveler: point of sale
daniel: oh. what's that?
FellowTraveler: so you can pay in a restaurant with your android phone
daniel: cool. no iphone?
FellowTraveler: no spyPhone yet. if someone is willing, sure. OT's open source, anyone could do it.
FellowTraveler: apple wouldn't allow it though, i'm pretty certain. app store == fascism
daniel: true
FellowTraveler: gotta go, meeting a guy who wants to open a gold-backed OT bank
daniel: bye
*You have left #agora

agora.io
=========

From: Caty <perfect10@mailvault.com>
To: Daniel LaRusso <daniel@mailvault.com>
Subject: funny kittens

hey danny boy,

we're doing a private viewing of the agora.io conference on the 25th. Dentons got a room set up at a restaurant and everything.
check out the speakers at http://agora.io

sincerely,
your princess

ps: MAKE SURE TO BRING FUN

***

As the train leaves the station, I watch the lights race past in the darkness. The reflections flicker in the window. The train leaves town and there are fewer and fewer lights. Finally, there exists only blackness outside my window. The main lights in the cabin are slowly dimming, until only the orange emergency lights and the green exit sign are visible. There is no one else in the wagon and I have my reading light switched off.

I press my forehead against the cold glass of the window, searching for lights far out in the landscape. Small towns race by, with maybe a few hundred lights. Bigger towns with thousands of lights. Islands of light in the darkness. From time to time, in the distance, I can see a city. The lit windows and streetlights and moving headlights blend together, forming a sea of light.

I've put my ticket on the table in front of me. I check once again if I brought everything. Wallet, phone, backpack with some clothes. Fun. Bring fun, she writes. The reflection of my face in the dark window shows me I'm smiling. I put in my earphones and play some laid back downtempo ambient to match the tranquility of the night. Princess, she writes. I don't know which I find more attractive: Her body or her craziness.

My mind starts wandering. Caty. Her pierced nose. Silver piercings. Silver. Currency. Money.

I suddenly realize that I'm trying to become a professional criminal. At least if I let myself be judged by the state. Avoiding taxes, disobeying regulations and laws. Trying to build an infrastructure and networks for likeminded people. I don't want to hurt anyone, but a government court would probably do us for conspiracy against the state. And all that because they rely on stealing from everyone, so anyone who doesn't pay up and obey is considered a criminal. It's dangerous to be right when the government is wrong.

When the conductor comes through to check my ticket, I suspect for a second she knows I'm am anarchist. But she smiles and I relax. I probably shouldn't become paranoid. The A-Team takes security very seriously. I chuckle to myself. A-Team, that's pretty good. I make a mental note to ask Denton about becoming paranoid. And about the A-Team.

Only a year ago, I'd have considered what I'm thinking now as criminal. Most people still would. But you can't let other people define you. They will define you in such a way that you must serve them. Denton's right. This is as much cultural as it is political. If every song, book and movie tells people to blindlessly worship authority, distrust themselves and their friends and hate money, trade and success, how could anyone be free? It takes a major disconnect from mainstream culture. As an anarchist, I'm on the fringe of "acceptable" culture. As an anarcho-capitalist, I'm in a minority even among anarchists. And agorism is a controversial and rare strategy even among anarcho-capitalists. Most anarcho-capitalists love talking about gold and Austrian Economics and how the state is unfair, but they don't actually want to do anything. Doing anything besides talking is illegal. They don't seem to realize that the rules are designed to keep them in check. If they don't break the rules, how will they break their chains?

I fall asleep thinking and dream of wondrous worlds, where people laugh about the idea of involuntary servitude. Where the idea of giving up freedoms to be safe sounds as ridiculous to everyone else as it does to me.

***

I take the bus. I hate public transportation. There aren't too many people riding the bus though. I survive. I have the address on my spyPhone and watch as the navigation software tries to give me turn-by-turn-directions, complaining every time the bus doesn't obey them. As the bus passes the address, I see Caty's piece of shit bicycle leaning against the building. My heart beats faster.

At the restaurant, I ask a waiter for the conference room. He directs me upstairs. The restaurant seems pretty empty, only a few late-lunchers here and there. The stairs are covered by a thick carpet that swallows every sound. I walk up the stairs in silence. At the top, there's a heavy wooden door. I pull it open and enter.

"Look who's late", Paul says. The room is huge. Almost the entire first floor. There's a projector focused on a large silver screen attached to a wall. The tables and chairs are set up facing the screen. The screen shows the http://agora.io website, but there's no talk going on yet. Paul is balancing his chair on two legs, leaning against the table behind him. Denton sits with his back to me. He's not wearing a robe this time, but a black dress shirt. There's a leather jacket on the back of his chair. He doesn't seem interested in turning around. Faust is leaning back in another chair, feet propped up on the table. I wonder if you're allowed to put your feet on the table in a restaurant. I guess you are if you rent the place. He's wearing a tie again, and a jacket. There's also a guy I've never seen - he's very tall, even sitting down, and he's wearing a Mises Institute polo shirt. Tu ne cede malis.

"Hi gang", I say.

"We're not a gang", explains Faust, "we're a movement."

"There doesn't seem to be alot of movement in the movement right now", I say.

"We're plotting", Faust says.

"I see", I say. The tall guy gets up and shakes my hand.

"I'm Max", he says.

"No you're not", I say. He smiles.

"Exactly. And you aren't Daniel?"

"I am Daniel", I say.

"Oh", he says, looking to Faust. Faust shrugs his shoulders. Max turns back.

"Well, it's nice meeting you, Daniel", he says.

I hear a toilet flush and a door open.

"What the fuck", Caty says from somewhere behind me, "I have to pee and he's here."

"Hi", I say, turning around. She's overwhelmingly hot. Her hair is tied back in a pony tail and then some. There's numerous things in there, holding together the matte black strains in a very tightly combed fashion. She's wearing grey sweat pants that are too wide for her. They hang on her hip, showing a lot of skin between the seam and her t-shirt. Her t-shirt says

"The price is right" and shows the supply and demand curves meeting. The silver ring in the wing of her nose looks exactly like I remember. She stands there, in the toilet door, not moving. As if she's waiting.

"You shouldn't do so much fairy dust", Denton says from the table, "you're probably just imagining him."

"I didn't do any fairy dust, you swine", Caty says, "what's with you and drugs?"

"Said the girl who snorted her bodyweight in cocaine", Denton says.

"I see you've met Mad Max", Caty says to me.

"Mad Max?", I say, "he didn't say he was mad."

"He isn't. It's a joke. It's like a lie, but it's funny. I invented it this morning", Caty says. She seems to find a lot of pleasure in taking credit for inventing language constructs.

"Anyway", she continues, "I like that you're nothing but a figment of my imagination. Makes everything easier." She comes closer, then really close. Then she punches me in the stomach.

"Ouch!", I say, "what'd you do that for?"

"No reason", she says. She walks to an empty chair and sits down. I just now see that there's a laptop in front of Denton and he's typing something.

"What's wrong with her?", I say to Mad Max.

"Everything", he says, and sits down at the table.

"What'd I miss?", I ask Denton, "and where's Michael?"

"Let me answer you in reverse order", Denton says, "Michael's in Singapore and you missed J. Neil Schulmann missing his time slot."

"The author of Alongside Night?", I ask

"Yes. Didn't show."

"Maybe he overslept", I offer.

"Maybe not", Denton says.

"So what's coming up next?", I ask. I've taken a glance at the schedule. There's three "channels", meaning three talks going on at all times, in parallel. One channel is dedicated to agorism, one to peaceful evolution and one to creative media. On the first day, this day, there's also a special fourth channel called the "AnCaps Entrepreneurship Network". I like this channel best from the titles.

"PorcLoom - A free currency for liberty loving members of the Free State Project in New Hampshire", says Denton, continuously typing on his laptop.

"What are you doing?", I say.

"Giving the speaker some last minute corrections on his crypto", Denton says.

"I see", I say.

"So Daniel", Mad Max says to me, "what's your deal?"

"What do you mean, my deal?", I say.

"What do you specialize in? What do you sell?", he says.

"I don't sell anything", I say.

"What?" He seems incredulous. "Why not?"

"I'm not sure. Why should I sell something?"

He looks around, as if to make sure I'm really there, really saying that. Am I an april's fools joke? It's august.

"Well", he says, "to make money, of course. How do you make your money?"

"I don't", I say, "just finished my degree. I should probably start selling something soon, you might be right."

"What is your degree in?", Max says.

"Have a wild guess", I say.

"Computer science", he guesses.

"Tada! You win", I say. We both chuckle.

"Kinda sad how all of the people in your movement are nerds", Caty says from somewhere behind me.

"Well, we have you", I say.

"That's right", Caty says, "I'm like the only person in this scene who isn't an angry white male computer programmer."

"You're pretty angry", Max says.

"I'll give you that", she says.

"And you're white", I say.

"Only in places you haven't seen yet", Caty says.

"I've seen you naked!", I say.

Caty says nothing. Max says nothing. Paul says nothing. Denton types away on his laptop.

"Sorry", I say.

"Awkward!", Faust says and laughs.

"Ok kids", Denton says and finally turns around. I can see a few open terminals on his laptop screen. Faust takes his feet off the table. Cathy hops closer on her chair. We've formed a semi-circle. I feel like I'm in grade school. We're missing the coloured ball we can throw at each other before we say our names and tell what we did last summer.

"I hope you've finished your blabber about who fucked who and which band is totally fab right now. I've set Michael up with another VPN in Singapore so he can watch the talks. He's up in the middle of the fucking night to see this. I hope you learn something from him. He's selling the WhisperPC to some businesspeople over there. He doesn't even speak the language yet. If he does it right, that's going to be hundreds of thousands of dollars worth of deals. And you sit here on my chairs and breathe my air. So why don't you get your shit together and DO something?", Denton says.

As if to release tension, the video channel on the silver screen starts moving and the sound system crackles.

"One-two, testing", says a voice. There's a chat next to the channel, and a few people type "we can hear you" or "seems to be working". A keynote slide appears on the screen. It says "PorcLoom" and has a golden coin featuring a porcupine next to it, the pet symbol of the Free State Project.

"Is it Bill?", I ask.

"No", says Denton.

"Didn't Bill write Loom?", I ask.

"No. But neither did this guy", Denton says.

"What did Bill write?", I ask.

"Bill wrote TruBanc and TruLedger", Denton says.

"Seems like everyone implements their own anonymous currency nowadays", I say.

The next slide appears. The speaker introduces himself as Alex Wied ("like the plant, haha") and gives a broad overview of PorcLoom. It seems exactly the same as Loom, just re-branded for FSPers. He gives a few use-cases. Then he explains the crypto-math. I've heard it all before, but I still blank out. I can't listen to this math crap. The guy says it's very unlikely that someone will crack the code. It's like hiding your money in a single atom in the universe and then guessing where to look for it. I believe him. Mostly because none of the other people in the room object. A few people in the chat claim Alex Wied lost them.

After explaining the cryptographical background, he closes Keynote and opens up Firefox. He opens PorcLoom.net. It looks pretty slick.

"Rails?", I guess. Denton types "rails?" in the chat.

"I started doing it in Rails, yea, but there were too many changes I had to make. In Rails they profess convention over customization, but PorcLoom is an unconventional project. I found myself fighting the framework, and as a result I switched to Sinatra on Rack", the speaker answers.

"Still a good guess", Denton says. I smile.

"Any questions?", the speaker asks.

"who r u on #agora?", 'michael69' types in the chat.

"What's #agora?", the speaker asks.

Denton smiles.

"Lady and gentlemen", he says ,"we have a winner! New guy, you're being promoted, this is the new new guy. What's your nickname again?"

"Daniel?", I say. Denton sighs and puts his face in his hand.

"Someone explain it to him again", he says.

***

"It just feels like lying", I say.

"So what? You're lying to protect yourself. If the state knows your name, they will lock you up", Faust says.

"I've just given up being an angsty teenager and accepting myself. Now I need to hide my real self again? This feels really weird!", I say.

"Look", Denton says, "you've been hearing all your life that your name is an integral part of your identity."

"Yea, I guess", I say, waiting.

"Yet you had zero influence on your name", he says.

"True", I say.

"And as a coder, you know that a name is nothing more than a descriptor of something, semi-unique enough for identification in certain namespaces and situations."

I think.

"Many names can point to the same thing or person. There are thousands of Daniels. Different persons or things can have the same names. A name might mean something completely different in another culture or another situation. You are 'Daniel' to your friends, but you're 'Mr. LaRusso' for the bank clerk. You're 'little brother' to your sister. You're 'that guy' to a cute girl you just met. You are 'sweety' to your girlfriend. You are 'new guy' for us, or at least you were."

"Yes", I say.

"So why do you find it so hard to use one more identifier, specific to a certain culture and situation?", Denton concludes.

"Hm", I say.

***

Patri Friedman has a talk on Seasteading (of course), but also about general anarchist activism and difficult methods of achieving liberty. His mapping of the evolution of libertarian thought to his family is interesting. Milton Friedman, his grandfather, was an economist. He believed in creating the right policy by informing the majority of people through debate and rational argument. David Friedman, Patri's father and one of the first proponents of anarcho-capitalism, recognized that the process of politics is rigged against libertarian policies, which is why rational argument and debate fail. He's a proponent of public choice theory, which Patri summarizes as 'politics doesn't work'. Still, Patri says, proponents of public choice and anarcho-capitalists of this generation try to influence people by debate and rational argument. As Patri says, it's writing a letter to the editor to explain why letters to the editor don't work. What kind of name is Patri, anyway? Is that his real name? I make a mental note to finally read David Friedman's Machinery of Freedom. The title makes a lot more sense to me now.

The third generation of libertarians, Patri explains, not only recognizes the need for another system of politics (or rather non-politics), like anarcho-capitalism. They also realize that the methods must be different. They can't rely on convincing a majority, on winning rational argument or debating. Rather, they need to create freedom for themselves and create competing systems on small scales, establish a market system by using the market itself. Imposing anarcho-capitalism from the top down? Crazyness. It would contradict anarcho-capitalism. Agorism, Patri recognizes, has accepted this markets-to-create-markets method.

Where Patri disagrees with agorism is the strategy. He thinks it's better to act in the open and compete with government through legal loopholes than to "hide and act like criminals". His main arguments for this are attracting funding, publicity and not attracting violent people and drug pushers.

"I have nothing against drug pushers", Caty says.

"I think he's wrong on one important count", Denton says.

"What's that?", I ask.

"He underestimates the state's willingness to just bomb the fuck out of him."

"Well", I argue ,"he said states usually don't attack other countries that compete with them openly, just when they launder money or sell drugs or harbour terrorists."

"Are you kidding me?", Mad Max says, "What did Britain do when the USA declared their independence? What did the Northern States do when the Southern States declared their independence? I'm pretty sure that every single effort to compete with an existing federal state has resulted in a war by said state."

"Plus", Paul says, "it's not like they really need you to harbour terrorists or do drugs or any of that. They'll just make it up, kill everyone and tell everyone the WMDs were there alright.."

"Hm", I say. I don't want to be bombed.

"Until I have a reasonable chance to defend myself against a standing army, I'd rather not try", Denton says, "Not that I'm not planning for it to happen."

"Plus, if they invested all that Peter Thiel money in some counter-economic business instead of floating platforms, they might have a massive effect right now instead of speculating that states won't nuke them", says Mad Max.

"Well, that's exactly his point, I think. Peter Thiel is afraid of being traced to counter-economics, because the state would take everything from him. It's easier to get money from the big guys if you're above ground", I say.

"I'd rather enable Peter Thiel to give me money in an untraceable way", Faust says, "the dude's loaded."

I want to be loaded too.

***

Sunday evening. The agora.io conference is almost over. Schulmann did get another time slot and had his talk. It was about adopting Alongside Night as a movie. Guess he's in the film business now.

"So when is your train going?", Caty asks. I stroke her hair slowly. Her head rests on my shoulder and she's curled up against me on the couch. The lights are dimmed and the others are watching the last talk.

"Eleven thirty", I say. Holding her, I realize how small she is. How thin and fragile. I want her to be happy. I want her to be safe. I want the world to be a safe and happy place for her. This is why I am an anarchist. This is why I'm doing this.

"What time is it?", she says into my shoulder. I'm pretty sure my t-shirt is ruined by now, she's been chewing and gnawing at it for at least an hour. My shoulder feels warm and wet.

"Ten o'clock", I say.

"Shit", she says, then: "You know, you could just stay here. You can sleep in my bed. You're done with your finals, right?"

"Yes, I'm done", I say.

"We could fuck", she says, as if sleeping in her bed wasn't enticing enough. I think. I don't really have a reason to go back yet. My room's empty, Tom's probably busy working on his online business thing. University's practically over. I don't even have to go get my degree, they're mailing it to me next week.

"Sure", I say. Caty gives me a kiss on the shoulder, through the hole in my t-shirt.

"Can you two get a room or something?", Faust says loudly from over at the screen, "I'm trying to watch this." I smile. Caty crawls over me, kneeing me in the balls in the process of standing up. I can hardly surpress my painful moaning.

"You're such a girl sometimes", Caty whispers and takes my hand, "come on!"

She pulls me in the bathroom.

WhisperPC
==========

Account Balance is: 0.00 BTC (0.00 USD @ 1.5229)

From: Tom Taylor <admin@moriartyconsulting.com>
To: N. M. Realname <nmrn@mailvault.com>
Subject: britney spears naked

hi whats going on?

i'm doing pretty wlel. i didn't even have to rent your room out to someone else, i make so much. you wouldn't believe how many people there are who're looking for untaxed work or want to hire untaxed workers. im close to 2k a month, diude. thats 2k before taxes and after taxes, cuz i dont pay any fucking taxes! and i only work like 40 hours. beat that, sucker! haha!1oneeleven

did you score with that chick? god, you're such a loser! (unless u did)
if she won't let you do her i can give you some money. maybe you can pay her for sex. haha!

tom

From: N.M. Realname <nmrn@mailvault.com>
To: Tom Tayler <admin@moriartyconsulting.com>
Subject: RE: britney spears naked

Hi,

I'm doing ok too. Not rich like you (yet). Trying to get into some business though. I not only scored with "that chick", I've moved in with her. She rapes me every night. She's a maniac. And I don't think your cute 2k/month would get you far with her, she's making way more than that ;-)

D.

***

"So let me set this up real quick", Michael says.

"I've seen one before", I say.

"Shut your mouth", Caty says, "we already know what a badass you are."

"Ok", Michael says, opening the WhisperPC and pushing the power button, "this thing's got all the new stuff. It's the final production version. Totally tricked out." The laptop is a nondescript, corporate-looking, black Lenovo. I wouldn't be able to tell it apart form hundreds of other corporate laptops. But I guess that's the point.

"See, you gotta have a password right in the beginning. There's nothing at all you can do with this thing, not even enter the BIOS, without entering a password. The hard drive is encrypted, too. So if someone steals your laptop and plugs the drive into another computer, he won't see shit."

"Cool", I say, "how much is it?"

"Depends on the spec. The cheapest mod we do is a $300 markup from the hardware. So if you order a $1000 laptop, it's $1300. Of course if you order some high end shit from Alienware or whatever, sky is the limit."

"But this is targeted at businesses, right?", Caty asks.

"Exactly", says Michael.

"So the specs don't matter at all", Caty says, "it just needs to be stable, reliable and secure."

"Exactly", says Michael.

"Don't you think businesspeople will want Windows?", I ask.

"I think if they want a secure machine, Windows is not an option. And this isn't really too different for the user. There's LibreOffice, Firefox and a few accounting apps. Most software is on all major systems anyway. It's not like they'll play video games on this thing."

"What's with communication?", Caty asks.

"Good question. There's Thunderbird with GPG preinstalled, of course. OpenVPN preconfigured. If you buy the premium package, it includes a one-year membership of encrypted Skynet VPN service. So you got your multi-hop VPN tunnel right there."

"And you think anyone will really buy this?", I say, "Why wouldn't they just buy a laptop and put all the software on it themselves?"

"Not everyone is so tech-savvy and not everyone wants to do that. You don't clean your own clothes and grow your own food. You probably could do it, but you got better things to do. Through economics of scale and specilization, some people just make more money doing other stuff for an hour than installing linux and downloading software", says Caty.

"Thank you, Caty", says Michael.

"Huh", I say.

"So your job, if you take it, will be to explain this to potential customers and sell it", Michael concludes.

"How much do we get?", I ask.

"10%", Michael says.

"So if I sell someone a $1300 laptop..", I speculate.

"..you get $130 from us", Michael says. My mind starts counting the money I will get.

"Just don't take a whole day to sell one", Caty says.

"Do you want one? See, it's matte black, like your hair!", I say to Caty.

"I already have one, douchebag", she says. Then she says to Michael:

"Do you sell a better brain for him?"

***

I sit in Caty's tiny apartment in her tiny kitchen on her one creaky chair and try to think. How I will market the WhisperPC. Who I will sell it to. Michael has given me a list of potential customers. I get up and fill the glass with tap water. Caty has literally one piece of everything. One glass, one fork, one knife, one spoon, one plate and one chair. I drink some water and sit on the chair again. On the table before me sits the WhisperPC Michael has given me.

The kitchen walls, like most walls in the apartment, are plastered with posters of naked women. Most of them are in black and white. They depict lithe girls lying on beaches, in beds, on meadows and car hoods. Some of them are spreading their legs, some are smiling, some look depressed and some look dreamingly into the distance. I keep wondering if Caty is a lesbian. Maybe she'll reveal to me one day she's been faking it all along and she doesn't even like guys and she'll laugh at me. Maybe not. Then again, I think, totally worth it.

Caty's out selling stuff. I'm not even sure she only sells precious metals and BitCoins. How many people are there that want to buy gold and silver and bits? It certainly isn't an everyday consumption good like bread.
I invent a really long and secure password for my demo WhisperPC. Then I pull out my spyPhone and spend 15 minutes connecting it to Caty's complicated stereo system. I'm not really that audio-savvy, but I recognize it's quite high quality. It has a dedicated amplifier, for fuck's sake. I put on Nlite and turn up the volume to what I anticipate to be a very loud but tolerable to neighbours level. I have to admit, the stereo system is very impressive.
I walk through the tiny apartment and can't hear anything but the music. No creaking when I sit in the chair, no squeaky floor boards, no noisy bed springs. I can't even hear the traffic through the open window. I sit in the kitchen between the WhisperPC and the naked girls, looking outside the window, watching the sun set. Hearing the music dance.

-Hello? Hello!?
Take your time.
Think about your next breath.
Appreciate that once again you've cheated death.
Realize there's nothing there to realize.
Every step don't have to lead to somewhere.
-Who is this?
Look to your left, see a friend beside you.

Look to your right, another there to guide you.
On your way where it is you stay,
wherever you get your head down.

***

The music has stopped. Probably for quite some time, as it is completely
dark now. I hear noise from the stairs. There is a bang against the door,
then I hear keys. Caty opens the door, bicycle under her arm. She's stronger
than she looks. Her slender body is all muscle and desire. I consider getting
up, but then stay in the chair. Caty throws her bike against the wall and
comes closer. She stops in the door frame to the kitchen, where the door is
missing. She grips the frame and stretches her limbs, yawning. Her right
pant leg is rolled up, like usual.

"So", she makes, "What have you been up to?"

"Nothing really", I say, "listening to some music. Thinking."

"What have you thought about?", she says and comes closer.

"You, me, money, you know", I say.

"Tell me", Caty says. She sits on my lap, since there's no second chair. Her
thighs are on mine and her ass hangs over the side, her back leaning against
the kitchen wall with the posters of naked girls.

"So one thing has come up again and again", I say. "Since you keep talking
about economics. I've been wondering. Is it unethical for me to pay you for
sex?"

Caty laughs.

"You're cute", she says.

"What do you mean?", I ask.

"First, you don't have any money to pay me for sex. Second, I already fuck
you without getting money."

"I'm thinking in principle. Is it unethical to pay for sex? I mean, if you love
the other person and such?", I say.

"What does that even mean, unethical?", Caty asks.

"You know", I say.

"I don't know, that's why I'm asking", Caty says.

"I mean if it is morally alright", I say.

"Oh come on, you don't believe in morals, do you?", Caty says, chuckling.

"Of course I do."

"Morals are bullshit. Morals are code for 'I like it'. There's nothing more to it than that. People consider moral what they would like others to do", Caty says.

"You're such a moral relativist", I say defensively.

"Yes, I am. I'm an everything relativist", Caty says.

"Don't you believe that some things are always immoral? Like murder and theft?"

"Of course. I, personally, believe you shouldn't murder and steal. But I don't pretend that it's anything more than my opinion", she says.

"But almost everyone believes that", I say.

"That makes it the opinion of almost everyone", Caty says.

"Don't you think some things should be true, not just opinions?"

"I don't care about should", Caty says, "I care about is. Whatever some people consider moral or ethical, it's obviously not binding for everyone. If it were, there wouldn't be murder or theft. So if it isn't binding, if it's just some idea in some people's head, how is it any different from an opinion?"

"So you're saying there is no should?", I ask.

"If there is should, it's in your head. And in mine. But it's a different should. If one day I'm not up for a fuck and you incentivise me with money, sure. I'm not convinced, though, that lack of money is what keeps most people from fucking."

"I'm still going to save", I say. Caty smiles.

"So I'm going to have a piss. You want to come?", she says, getting up from my lap.

"Maybe another time", I say. She's halfway to the toilet when I shout after her.

"Hey Caty", I say.

"Yea?", she says and smiles.

"Have you done any drugs today?", I ask.

Caty rolls her eyes and turns away.

I hear her steps on the wooden floor and then the bang of the toilet door. She turns the key in the lock and I sit in silence. Waiting for her. Again.

Cannoneer's Farm
==================

"This guy's high profile. He's like the CEO of a large network of agorist farms", Caty says.

"'Like'?", I ask.

"Since it's not technically a corporation, he's not technically a CEO, just a boss", Caty says.

"Where are we meeting him?"

"He's a little paranoid, even by our standards", Caty says, "He wants to meet at a neutral location and then take us to his farm blindfolded, to make sure we can't rat him out."

"Blindfolded?", I ask.

"Yea", she smiles, "kinky, huh?"

"I don't know, that sounds really weird. What if he kidnaps us?", I say.

"No risk, no fun", Caty says. "Besides, two kidneys are overrated."

"We could track the position with a GPS phone", I say.

"I'm pretty sure they'll search us", Caty says.

"You just want to get blindfolded!", I say.

She laughs.

"Maybe, and earn some money at the same time. Plus, he's doing some kind of special dinner party this weekend. We're supposed to bring fancy clothes", she says.

"Shit", I say, "I don't have any fancy clothes."

"Don't worry. I have to get mine from my parents' house anyway. I'm sure you can borrow some from my brother."

"You have a brother? You have parents?", I say.

"What did you expect?"

"I don't know, I just never thought about it. Maybe someone made you in their own image", I say.

"Made me? Out of what?", she says.

"Out of crazy and porn tapes", I say. Caty shakes her head.

"You're unbelievable", she says, "I hope you've started saving."

***

I'm extremely nervous. Caty rings the doorbell. The house looks really upscale. The door buzzes and Caty walks in. I take a look at the sign. "Dähnhardt", it says. Judging from the 7 Series BMW her parents are pretty loaded.

"Oh honey, I'm so glad to see you", shrieks a woman with black hair in maybe her 40s. Must be Caty's mother. She topples towards us in extremely high heels that look very uncomfortable. She's wearing a tight skirt that doesn't seem to allow much freedom of movement for her knees. She makes very small steps.

Caty hugs her and they kiss each other on the cheeks. Then I get hugged and kissed on the cheek. I kind of kiss on the cheek back, but I don't dare to hug this twig of a woman, in fear of breaking her. A balding man with large glasses and a grey beard stands in a doorway. Must be the father. When the hugging is done, he comes over. He's dressed in a suit and wears very shiny black shoes. His left hand stays in his pocket as he shakes my hand. His handshake is dry and firm. He's a little taller than me.

"And you must be..", he begins.

"Daniel", I say, forgetting to use my pseudonym. Then again, maybe it's appropriate to use my real name here.

"Ah, Daniel, of course. So good to finally meet you", he says.

"You too", I say.

He takes me by the shoulder and leads me through a high doorway into a large dining room. The furniture looks old and expensive. There's a fucking crystal chandelier on the ceiling. Dinner is being served by a young man and an older woman. I am advised to sit next to Caty, facing her father on the other side of the very long table. Next to him sits the mother, facing Caty herself.

"So, how are your studies going?", the father asks.

"Excellent. I spend all day in the library, studying", Caty says, "in fact, I met Daniel at the library."

Her father nods approvingly.

"What do you study, Daniel?", he asks.

"Computer science", I say. This is the best cover-up ever. Ask me questions about algorithms & data structures, I dare you!

"Ah, a scientist!", he says.

"More of a programmer", I say and take a drink from my water.

"I didn't know you were into nerds, Marie", says the mother.

MARIE? I spew a mouthful of water on the table and cough. Caty, -- or rather, Marie?, claps my back.

"You ok?", she asks.

"Why, Marie", I cough, "I'm excellent, thank you."

"He's not really a nerd. See, he doesn't wear any glasses", Caty/Marie says to her mother.

"Your father wears glasses and he isn't a nerd either", the mother says.

"Just because he can't use a computer doesn't mean he isn't a nerd", Caty/Marie says, "admit it mom, you like nerds!"

"I guess you got it from someone", the mom chuckles.

"Marie", I say, "where's the bathroom? I have to relieve myself of some baggage, I'm afraid."

"Oh, do you have to puke? Come on, I'll show you", she says and gets up. I follow her out of the room and we walk past the young man who served dinner. He's just standing there, waiting, I guess. We get to the bathroom and Marie locks the door behind us.

"What the fuck", I say, "Marie?!"

"If you don't like it, just call me Caty", she says.

"That's totally not the point!"

"What is the point then? That I didn't tell you my real name? Boohoo, you big crybaby. Water is wet, the sky is blue, girls have secrets."

"You could have warned me", I say, "I almost spit in your fathers face."

"Oh, come on, it was funny", she says.

"And what's with the university?"

"Just go along with it. Don't tell them I snort cocaine. Don't tell them I sell gold for cash on the street at night. Don't tell them about Denton. Oh, yea, don't tell anyone else my real name. Can you do that?", she says.

"I'll try", I say, "any other secrets I should know about? Are you a robot?"

"I'm a superhero, but not a robot", she says and gives me another clap on the back. I cough once more. She unlocks the door and walks back. I follow her, shaking my head. Crazy bitch.

***

Caty or Marie opens her brother's wardrobe and goes through the suits. He has lots of suits.

"So what should I call you? Caty? Marie?", I ask, sitting on her brother's bed. It's pretty soft and comfy.

"Call me Mother Theresa if you like", she says. She's really downplaying this, as if it were no big deal.

"I'm serious. How can I ever call you Caty again, knowing it isn't your real name? But I can't call you Marie in front of the others. What kind of name is that, anyway? Marie Dähnhardt? What are you, from the middle ages?"

"Yes", she says, grabbing a suit, "I told you I'm a princess."

"Fuck you", I say.

"In a minute", she says, "now try on this suit. You're about as tall as my brother, so this should fit."

I strip down my pants and put on the silky-feeling dress suit pants. I don't dare to move quickly, afraid of ripping holes in them. How can anyone walk around in these? She makes me put on a dress shirt and ties a tie around my neck. Then the jacket. The jacket is rather loose compared to the pants.

"You should see my brother", she says, "he's built."

When I'm all dressed up, we go to her old room. Her closet is full of girly dresses. She knows what she's looking for and quickly pulls out two elegant dresses. One black, one white. She puts them down on the bed, on which I again sit.

"So did you lose your virginity on this bed?", I ask her. She pulls her pants down and steps out of them. The muscles play under her bronze skin as she makes a little step towards me and grabs the black dress.

"No", she says, stepping in the dress, "but I know about a dozen boys who did." She turns around and motions for me to zip up the back of the dress. This feels very medieval to me. Clothes that can't be completely put on by a single person? Who makes stuff like that? As I slowly pull up the zipper, I watch the bony line in the middle of her back dissappear from view inside the dress. There's still plenty of skin to be seen. I guess that's the point of elegant dresses: an excuse to look like a hooker. Not that she needs an excuse. She turns around on her tip toes and the seam of the dress flies around her, making woosh sounds. She then takes a jewelery case out of the closet and inserts a pair of pearly earrings into her earlobes.

"You look beautiful", I say to her. She's beaming.

"You're not too unfuckable either, Mr. All Serious And A Tie", she says and smiles.

"This is just your way of boning your brother, isn't it", I say. She pushes me on the bed and jumps on me.

"Wait!", I say, "I'll rip the stupid suit." She waits patiently as I take off the suit pants, jacket, tie and dress shirt. Then she pushes me on the bed again. She keeps the black dress on. The bottom is so wide open it doesn't really matter anyway. The black dress flies around me. The princess Marie Dähnhardt fucks me on her childhood bed like a crazed teenager.

***

A little later, she goes to the toilet to squirt out the spunk, still in the black dress. Meanwhile, I carefully put the suit into a bag she has brought. When she's done, she puts both dresses and the earrings in the bag and we leave.

She kisses her mom and dad goodbye and waves.

"Visit us sometime, sweety", the mom shouts after us.

"I just did, mom", Marie shouts back.

"Visit us again", mom shouts.

"Maybe next semester, I have lots of classes right now", Marie shouts. I wave to her parents.

Five minutes later we arrive at the subway station and she's ceased being Marie. She has become Caty again. She expertly spits in a trash can and stabs me in the stomach with her pointy index finger. Even her pants leg is rolled up again. I didn't even see her do it.

***

"I'm sorry, but this is necessary for our protection", one of the thugs in dark suits says. At least he doesn't pretend it's for our protection, like the thugs in blue do.

No shit, they're really blindfolding us.
One of the guys has taken my phone and searched my wallet. Should've guessed no spyPhones were allowed on Cannoneer's farm. Another guy pulls out the black cloth and tells Caty to close her eyes. He then pulls the cloth over her face and makes a knot behind her head. She turns around slightly and almost stumbles. The guy grabs her arm to steady her, but she shakes him off. He takes another blindfold and I close my eyes.

They guide us a few steps to a car. They have to help us up into the car and we sit in the back seat. SUV. The doors clap in a very solid fashion, almost a "thunk". Definitely not a cheap car. The seats are perforated leather, real leather from the smell of it. When the driver starts the engine, I start guessing.

"Land Rover?", I say.

Nobody answers.

"Definitely a V8", I go on, "and the turning signal doesn't sound like a Mercedes."

Someone sighs close to me and it isn't Caty. I can hear her breathing lightly to my left. I sneak my hand over the expansive leather back seats and find her thigh. She grips my hand with hers and squeezes it. Her skin feels very warm.

"So", I conclude, "it's a Range Rover V8. Probably not the Sport, you guys don't look like cheapskates. The suspension isn't quite up to German standards. Do you feel the vehicle roll in the corners? You should've gotten the ML with air suspension."

"Can you please make your boyfriend shut up?", says a voice from the front seat, maybe the driver.

I smile under my blindfold. Then Caty's hand lets go of mine and crawls up my arm. She finds my neck and pulls me closer. I hear the click of her seatbelt release. There's nothing for a second. Then I wince as she climbs on me, kneeling in reverse over my legs. I can feel how close her face is. Her hot breath penetrates my blindfold as she searches for my face in the darkness. She gives me a kiss on the forehead. Then one on the chin. She hits my mouth on the third try and I don't talk about cars for the rest of the drive.

***

They probably didn't have to use any fancy driving techniques. I can't even tell if we drove for minutes or hours. The bottom of my blindfold is soaked in girl spit and my legs are numb from Caty's weight. We're finally helped out of the back seat. There's gravel under my feet. One of the guys warns Caty as she steps down from the car. The car speeds away and I never find out if it's really a Range Rover.

"Alright", the head thug says, "I'll take off your blindfolds now. Please excuse the inconvenience."

I'm surprised how dark it is already. The sun has started setting and barely peeks over the woods. We're near woods. Interesting. I roll my head and stretch my neck muscles, all thuggish, too. They've taken us to a big farm style mansion. The gravel driveway we're on disappears into said woods a few hundred meters from the house. There are lights on in the house, but I can't really see inside. The windows are tinted, and while light escapes, it's not clear what's going on.

The head thug hands me our clothes bag and makes an inviting gesture towards the mansion. Caty takes the lead and, with still sleepy legs, I follow her up the stairs. Before I step inside, I take a deep breath. I don't smell any animal shit in the air. Isn't this supposed to be a farm?

Inside, a waiter type in a white dinner jacket and a black bowtie is expecting us.

"This way, please", he says and makes a pulling gesture, as if to suggest we follow him.

I'm skeptical, but Caty seems to be enjoying the whole classy act. It's probably her aristocrat blood. Dancing on balls, wearing bowties - she was literally bred for this shit! Generations upon generations of blue blooded evolution have wiped out even the last traces common sense and humbleness from her gene pool. She's a purely-bred, finely-tuned eye-pleaser, designed and made to make minds orgasm on sight. It's working.

White dinner jacket man shows us to a large bedroom with its own bathroom attached. There's a huge bed with a card on it that says "Welcome to Buccaneers's Den, Mr. and Mrs. N. M. Realname." I laugh and show Caty the card.

"They think we're married", I say.

"This can be our honeymoon", Caty says, hops on the bed and pulls her shirt over her head, "are you coming?"

"Now? What's wrong with you? We're supposed to go down to the ball thing", I say.

"I'm not making out with you in the fucking car to eat shrimps and caviar all night", she says, "either you're cooling me down or I'll have to stuff a bunch of ice cubes down there."

***

After she's done she goes in the shower. I explore the room a little. There's a bible in the night stand and candles and matches on top. The heavy curtains are fastened to the walls, as to let light into the room. The sun has now completely set and I see only a few lights out in the darkness. There's no lighting in the driveway, only what seems like torches on the porch. They must've lit them after we've arrived.

Caty comes from the shower like a piece of art, her stomach and her thighs are liquid bronze. She stands before me for a second and puts her hands on her hips. Then she scratches her neatly mowed pubes.

"You keep giving me crabs", she says and laughs at me like that's super funny.

"Just imagine I said something clever about your promiscuity", I say and go shower.

***

When I'm done showering, she's turned herself into Marie. Black dress swooshing around her legs, hair all fixed up with some sticks, shiny pearl earrings in her ear lobes. She's even removed the ring in her nose.

"Marie?", I say.

"Could've fooled you, right?" Marie beams like a crazy person full of happy.

"You can't tell any of them my real name, though. You get that, right?", she asks in a serious tone.

"Sure", I say, "I understand it. Let's just hope I don't have a little slip up."

"I'll divorce you right there", Caty says, "with a knife. From your dick."

"Ok, calm down", I say.

"I'm serious. Keep your shit together. This is important", Marie says.

She helps me put on the tie and takes my arm.

"Why don't we go downstairs and join the festivities, Mrs. Realname?", I say.

"Why, I would love to, Mr. Realname", says Marie.

***

"Have you met Ma- my lovely wife?", I say. Fuck. Second guy and I'm already slipping up.

Marie lets the guy kiss the back of her hand. He puts on the perfect gentleman act and she does the lady. I watch rather passively. They exchange compliments and I scan the room. There's a long dinner table being set by a bunch of people in white dinner jackets wearing bowties, like the guy who showed us our room. In fact, I think he's among them. A few people are standing around in small groups and talk. I count about 20 plates on the table. There are snacks (what are they called? endeuvres?) on another table next to the wall. I could eat something, I realize. I turn to Marie.

"Ma- my love, would you excuse me for a second? I would rather enjoy filling myself up with some snacks", I say.

"Certainly, N.M.", Marie says. I see in her eyes I should probably try not to fuck up again.

"What does N.M. stand for?", the gentleman asks me.

"Nestor Machno", says Marie. I thought it stood for Not My, as in Not My Realname. I was thinking about Tim Realname, as in This Isn't My Realname. But N.M. sounds classier. The gentleman laughs heartily.

"Nestor Machno at a dinner party", he says, "that's brilliant." He shakes my hand and I gravitate towards the snacks. I stuff myself with fishy cream bread and cheese on toothpicks. The cheese is pretty good. Kind of exotic. Maybe goat milk. I hope there's no funny surprise food at this dinner. I don't want to eat cheese with maggots or monkey brain.

When I return, Marie has attracted numerous other gentlemen and a few ladies as well. They're standing around her in a half-circle like a bunch of raptors. Marie is saying something and everybody laughs. One guy even slaps his thigh. Wow. I examine the lady closest to my age. She's probably around 35, but I'm bad with people's ages. She too is wearing a black dress. Not as short and wide as Marie's, more like the tight thing Marie's mother wore earlier. It shows off her figure nicely. However old she is, she has very nice curves. In fact, she's like the antithesis of Marie. Long blond hair in a bun behind her head. Her boobs are probably a D cup, deep cleavage and her ass sways nicely when she shuffles her feet around. Where Marie's natural tan gives her an exotic, dark complexion, this woman has creamy white skin that goes very well with her large tits. I try to compare the two of them by numbers, but they're both 10s in their own, different ways. I feel like a douchebag even thinking that. Sounds like beautiful unique snowflake talk. I man up by telling myself I'd love to have a threesome with the two of them. Problem solved.

"I haven't introduced you to my handsome husband, have I? Nes, darling, why don't you come over here and meet these nice people", Marie shouts to me. Nes? Way to go, Anarchy. I walk next to her and penetrate the raptor half circle. She takes my arm and lays her head on my shoulder. All the while she continues making conversation with one or more of her new friends. I shake some hands. I shake the blonde's hand. I'd love to give her some cheek kisses, but she keeps her distance, just listening in. From time to time, when she is involved in conversation, I take longing looks into her deep cleavage. There's a mole right down the center on the left tit. Why do women always have moles in their cleavages? It's a conspiracy, I'm sure of it.

Marie kicks me in the shin.

"Aww, what was that for?", I say.

"Don't be rude to our host, Nes, he's asked you a question!", Marie says. I turn to the guy facing me. This is our host Cannoneer? He looks much less piratey than I expected. He's a bit taller than me and has little hair left on his head. He's probably in his 50s. He's a little fat but very muscular underneath. Probably did a lot of hard physical work and then moved to a desk job. It might be his past as a pirate. I hear sailors are ridiculously muscular. I want to shake his hand, but he indicates we have already shook hands. Fuck. I hope Marie's orgasmic laugh and her exposed skin distract him from my social awkwardness.

"What was the question?", I ask him.

"I was wondering if you chose the nym of Nestor Machno due to his legendary historic experiments in implementing anarchism over large areas of the Ukraine, or if you merely refer to him as a symbol of direct action, in fact propaganda of the deed or walking the walk, as could be said."

I stare at him blankly. I barely knew Nestor Machno was from the Ukraine.

"I like his beard", I say.

Cannoneer laughs, and so do most of the raptors. And Marie. She pats my cheek, then steps on her tip toes to reach up and kiss me.

"I'm glad you didn't bring your beard", she says, "it makes you all scratchy."

"It's called being a man", I say.

"I still hail the inventor of the razor blade", Marie says. I consider making a comment about razors and her pubes, but decide this is probably the wrong setting. I should work on my sense of context. Since I don't say anything, Cannoneer grasps the opportunity.

"Nes, it's a pleasure for me to introduce you to my wife Michelle", says Cannoneer. The hot blonde steps forward and I can barely keep my gaze from wandering down into the shaking abyss of her cleavage.

"The pleasure is all mine", I say. I realize I've been staring at her for too long and they expect me to say something.

"She's fascinating", I say. Cannoneer laughs and seems not at all jealous. Michelle the blond tit monster smiles. If she only knew I want to bone her tits, she wouldn't be smiling. Or would she? Maybe-

"Will I have to chain you to the bed tonight, Nes?", Marie says. I turn to her and blink.

"What? No, that won't be necessary. Probably."

"He's adorable", Marie says to Cannoneer and Michelle. Then she pulls my head down, gives me a kiss on the cheek and whispers in my ear.

"I won't be mad if you fuck her", she whispers.

I look up to see if Cannoneer or his trophy wife have heard her, but it doesn't appear so. They're watching in glee as the cute young girl kisses her husband on the cheek.

"Uh, thanks, Ma- Mrs. Realname, I mean, honey", I say, "maybe another time."

"Looks like dinner is served", Cannoneer says and gestures for us to move to the table. He leads the way, holding hands with Michelle. Michelle's ass sways back and forth beneath the thin fabric of her black dress and I wonder if she's wearing any panties underneath and if she shaves her pussy.

I turn to Marie and see her watching me. I try to decipher her face, but she's too good at this.

"Sorry", I say.

"Don't be sorry. I don't care if you fuck around", says Caty.

"For real?"

"If you like humungous boobs and blondes, what can I really do?", she says.

"Be honest", I say, "are you mad right now? I can't tell. Really."

"No", Marie says, "I'm not mad. I'm jealous of her boobs."

"Aww, come on. Don't feel bad. I'm sorry. I totally adore you, you know that", I say.

"Let's just eat something", Marie says and turns towards the dinner table, "maybe I'll put on some fat in the right places."

Her little tush makes the seam of her dress dance with every step as I follow her.

***

I put my suit pants on a chair and loosen the tie enough to pull it over my head.

"Let's talk about this", I say to Caty, who's standing semi-naked in the bathroom, scrubbing her teeth.

"What do you want to talk about?", she says inbetween brushing and spitting. I watch her chest as she bows down to rinse her mouth.

"Oh, come one", I say, "is this where we don't talk about stuff and get all upset and then start to hate each other?"

"I guess it is", she says and walks out of the bathroom. The black dress lies on the floor at her feet, and she kicks it.

"What happened to Ms. Love is Economics? Come on, walk me through this." I crawl beneath the thick blanket and my head disappears in the cushions. Caty flicks out the light. I feel the bed springs give way as she enters the bed. I stare at the ceiling and see dark shadows and nothing else. I expect her to come closer and hug me or something, but she doesn't. I sneak my hand towards her under the blanket and find her back turned to me. I massage the bony peaks of her spine with my fingertips, then let my hand climb over her ribs and towards her tits. I'm afraid she'll push me away, but she doesn't. Instead, she takes my hand and hugs it to her chest closely.

"This sucks", she says, "I know what the right thing is, but that doesn't make it easy."

"I thought there was no 'right thing'", I say.

"The right thing for what I want", says she.

"What do you want?", I ask.

"At the moment, you."

"But you have me", I say. With her hands pressing my fingers to her chest, I can feel her heartbeat.

"You like blondes with double-Ds, right?", she asks.

"I also like you", I say. She sighs.

"Come on, don't bullshit me. Right now, in this moment, would you prefer if I had big tits?"

Don't. Don't. Don't. No.

"Yes", I say.

"See", she says, and her voice is muffled by the cushion, "and I'll never have big tits. I could probably get plastic surgery or some other extreme shit, but there would still be desires you have that I could not fulfill. Imagine I got a boob job and you suddenly remember how you liked me before. Would I need to get my boob job undone? It's absurd to expect one person to fulfill every desire and every whim another has." Now I see where she's going with this.

"So you're saying I should sleep around?" She sighs again.

"That's the hard part, yes. I'm saying if there is a desire you have that I can not fulfill, it would be stupid of me to demand that you not fulfill it, and be it with someone else."

"Selfish maybe, but stupid?", I say.

"I don't give a fuck about selfish. I mean counterproductive. If my goal is to maximize my happiness with you, I think preventing you from doing what you want is not going to help me. Even if it makes me feel better in the short term. Maybe this time, I could stop you from banging the blonde. But next time you wouldn't tell me. Or you'd start resenting me and giving me a hard time about everything. Or something else."

"You're making a very good case for why I should fuck Titdzilla", I say. Caty doesn't chuckle. I don't think she even smiles, but I can't see her face.

"Yes. And while I rationally believe that's my best strategy, it's still difficult for me to accept", she says.

"So it's a time preference thing?", I ask. She laughs.

"Exactly", she says.

"You prefer the future pleasure of enjoying me to the immediate gratification of having me all to yourself?", I ask.

"Yes", she says.

"So you're investing in me. I'm your capital. That's fucked up!", I say.

Her whole ribcage vibrates as she laughs.

"What if we got married?", I say. She turns around and pushes my hand away, staring at me.

"What?!"

"I said-", I begin.

"I heard what you said, asswipe. I don't understand WHY you would say that. Did you even listen to me?", she says.

"But then you wouldn't have to worry about that kind of stuff", I say.

"You're such an idiot! Haven't I taught you anything?", she says, "Marriage is for cowards."

"But Denton's married, and so is Cannoneer", I say defensively.

"Listen to me, Daniel LaRusso. I will NEVER marry you. I repeat: never." I look away to avoid her stare. I'm not sure if I should be offended. I sure feel rejected, but I'm also confused. I feel my eyes get wet and blink.

"Why not?", I manage.

"Because I love you", she says.

"I don't understand", I say.

"Marriage is effectively a legal monopoly on another person's love. What have I told you about monopolies?"

"You can't be serious", I say, "you don't want to marry me because it's uneconomical?"

"Yes", Caty says, "if we get married, we won't have as big an incentive to fulfill each other's desires and needs. Because we don't have to. The other person can't just leave or take a better offer."

"What if we try really hard?", I ask.

"You should really read David Friedman", Caty says, "your public choice is awful. Incentives work, no matter how hard you try to ignore them. I would get fat and puffy and I'd stop shaving my pussy. You'd fart in bed and not shave and leave your dirty socks on the floor. Besides, what would I do with my legal monopoly on your cock? Sue you every time you're hot for a blonde with a rack? How's that going to stop your attraction to blondes?"

It's my turn to sigh.

"So we will never get married?", I say.

"No. Never", Caty says and gives me a kiss, "but that just means we'll try harder."

I stick my tongue out and try to put it into her mouth.

"All this econ talk is making me horny", I say, "are we going to fuck or what?"

Caty smiles.

We fuck.

***

"I'm a country boy, in theory at least", I say to Cannoneer, "but I don't think I've ever been on a farm for more than an hour."

"You're welcome to get your hands dirty anytime", says Cannoneer.

"Why doesn't your farm stink?", I ask. Caty chuckles.

"If you smell shit, the animals probably smell shit. If the animals have to live in their own shit smell, it's probably not a healthy farm", Cannoneer says.

"But almost all farms smell like shit", I say. Cannoneer says nothing.

"I see", I say. We walk past a group of cows that graze on some tasty grass.

"This is what Joel Salatin calls 'Salad Bar Beef'", Cannoneer says, "It's cheaper than feeding them with grains. The grass just grows here. And they make their own fertilizer."

"Maybe the shit smell isn't in the air because the shit goes into the grass", I speculate. Cannoneer stops and looks at me.

"You're exactly right", he says, "you should become a farmer!" I smile. Caty laughs at me.

"What?", I say to Caty, "I'd make an excellent farmer."

"You'd have to get up early", she says.

"Is that true?", I ask Cannoneer.

"Depends on what you mean by farmer", Cannoneer says, "if you want to WORK on a farm, you have to get up very early. Milk the cows. Put them out on the pasture. Collect the eggs. But I don't do all that myself anymore. I pay people to do it. I can sleep in."

"Do you sleep in?", I ask.

"No", Cannoneer says.

"So you're not a farmer, you just invested in a farm?", Caty asks.

"Well, I started out working on a farm. Then I bought a farm and worked on it. Then I hired people to do the work for me. I think that's actually a very natural and healthy progression, it's a shame more people don't do it", Cannoneer says.

"It's probably the government's fault", I say.

"Of course", Caty says, "by increasing the barrier to entry, states prevent people from joining the capital market freely. Instead, they have to slave away until they're old enough to retire. And the state steals all their savings via social insecurity, taxes and inflation. Without the state, everybody could just invest their money in their own business."

"How many cows do you have?", I ask Cannoneer.

"On this farm?", he says.

"Oh", I say, "I didn't realize you had several farms."

"A few", Cannoneer smiles.

***

"I'll take it", says Cannoneer. I'm kind of dumbfounded. First, he's buying it way too quickly. Second, he's only buying one?

"Uh", I make.

"Give the man his laptop, Nes", Caty says. I hand Cannoneer the WhisperPC. He waves one of his goons closer and hands him the laptop.

"How much did you say is it?", he asks.

"$1300", I say. Cannoneer opens his wallet, takes out a few bills, counts them, and hands them over.

"Thanks", I say and take the money. It's $1300. I put it in my pocket.

"Thank you", says Cannoneer.

***

Head thug drives us back to Berlin. Blindfolded. In Caty's tiny apartment, I start calculating.

"We made $300 in two days, that's $75 per person per day", I say, "that's not very good, is it?"

Caty shakes her head.

"You're such an idiot. This wasn't about that single WhisperPC. We sold him on the idea. If he likes it, he'll take a few dozen. And he'll tell his friends about it."

"Maybe we can get his wife to join #agora", I say, "I want to cybersex her."

"Haha, in your dreams", Caty says and smiles.

Jail
=====

From: Tom <admin@moriartyconsulting.com>
To: Daniel <daniel@skynet.com>
Subject: .

you ok? your never in icq any more. i got 3 employees now. working sucks, anyway. they do everything for me. some guys in the philipines. im thinking about traveling. maybe australia. bitcoin just passed $3 this morning. crazy. that means its 2x the euros value.

tom

From: Daniel <daniel@skynet.com>
To: Tom <admin@moriartyconsulting.com>
Subject: Re:.

yea i'm ok. very busy lately. i got into selling laptops! have to tell you about it sometime.
we've sold over 50 units last month. pretty sweet, huh?
have to share profits with caty though. then again, she does most of the selling.

daniel

***

I hit cruise control and the car glides forward at a constant 80km/h.

"Don't speed", Caty says, "this isn't a highway."

"+20 is ok", I say, "they have to deduct 3km/h and up until 20 over the limit you only pay like 30€."

"Maybe this isn't the right time to get pulled over", Caty say. She has her knees pulled up and against the dashboard. Her head is propped up against the passenger side window and she stares out into the dark night.

"Why, are you drugged up again?", I say.

Caty doesn't say anything.

"I said, are you-"

"I heard what you said, asshole", Caty says.

"And?", I say and change lanes.

"And I don't feel like taking shit from you right now", Caty says.

"I don't get it", I say. She hesitates.

"What don't you get?", she asks after a few moments of silence.

"Why you do it", I say, "cocaine, I mean."

"It has nothing to do with you", she says.

"Denton was right, I guess." Caty gets upright in her seat and turns to me.

"With what?", she asks.

"Forget it", I say.

"Tell me now", she says.

"He said you can't even look me in the eye and say you haven't done drugs today."

"Are you kidding me?"

"Can you?", I say and look over to her. She rolls her eyes and turns away.

"If you haven't, why can't you just say it?", I ask.

"WATCH THE FUCKING ROAD", she screams. I snap my head forward and there's a car directly in front of us. I swerve to the left, barely missing the left bumper with my rental car. I brake and the display says "Cruise Control Off". Fuck! I'm such an idiot. On cruise control and not watching the road. Lucky.

"SHIT", Caty screams, "It's a cop!"

And indeed, there's a blue light flashing in the mirror. A red LED panel lights up, reading "Polizei, bitte anhalten". I slow down and set the right turning signal.

"Great job, asshole, you almost hit the fucking cops! We're fucked!", Caty screams at me.

"It wouldn't be a problem if you weren't such a junkie", I shout. I bring the car to a stop on the side of the road. The cop car pulls up behind us and turns the blue flashing lights off. I kill the engine.

"You're unbelievable", Caty says and looks me straight in the eyes, "I haven't done any drugs in almost two weeks. But we're loaded up on WhisperPCs and we have tens of thousands of Euros in cash on us."

She's right.

"We sold most of the WhisperPCs", I say. Caty doesn't answer. She pulls out her aPhone and hits speed dial.

There's a knock on my window. I turn around. I can only see a dark figure standing out there. I hit the window controls and the window slides down.

"License and registration, please", says the cop. I turn towards Caty and open the glovebox. There's another cop standing at her door, aiming his flashlight inside and at the glovebox. What is this shit, are they afraid I'm going to pull a gun out? I get the registration and hand it to the cop.

"Hey", Caty says into her phone, "we've been stopped by the cops."

"Please turn off your phone, mam", says the cop. Caty completely ignores him. I pull out my wallet and hand the cop my drivers license.

"Ok", Caty says, then, "thank you."

The cop shines his light at Caty.

"I said, please turn off your phone, mam", he repeats. Caty gives him an "I dare you" look, then puts the aPhone back in her pocket.

"Don't say anything but your name", Caty says to me, "I mean it. Nothing. Everything's going to be alright."

She relaxes in her seat and grabs my hand.

"Please step out of the car, sir", the cop says. I look at Caty and she smiles.

***

"Don't make this harder on yourself than it needs to be", says the cop. We've been transported to a police station in the back of the cop car. The second cop drove my rental, following us.

"You want some coffee?", the cop says and offers me a cup. I hate coffee.

"Are you the good cop?", I say.

"Shut up", Caty says.

"Now, you shouldn't talk your boyfriend into trouble, young lady", the cop says. He isn't much older than I am, I guess. Maybe 30 or 35. Short hair, fit looking. He probably believes he's the good guy.

I don't say anything. Caty doesn't even look at him.

"I'm trying to be nice here, guys", says Good Cop, "when my partner comes back and sees you're giving me shit, he's not going to be so soft on you."

I burst out laughing. But I keep my mouth shut. Caty giggles.

***

"You're going to jail for this", says Bad Cop. I focus on a black spot on the wall across the room.

"Almost twenty thousand euro worth of stolen merchandise", Bad Cop says, "plus the cash. That's some hard time right there. The judge will add disobeying an officer, of course."

I stare at the spot. Bob the spot, I call him.

"The lowest sentence for that kind of crime is 3 years", he says, "that means you're not going in with the nice guys. You're going in with the hard boys. And your pretty little girlfriend here.." He laughs. I wonder if Bob the spot has any friends and scan the wall around him. Oh, there they are. Bob has a female looking spot right next to him. I call her Alice. Then there's Charlie the spot a little lower. Charlie the spot was probably Bob's best man.

"-Lesbians!", says Bad Cop. He said something before that, but I didn't listen. Lesbians got my attention.

"Got your attention now, huh?", Bad Cop says grimly. "The thought of some manly dykes ganging up on your precious little girlfriend, maybe giving her a little love, hu?" My thoughts immediately turn to lesbian porn. I'm not sure Bad Cop's tactic is working in his favour. He continues talking, but my thoughts drift off to naked, sweating whores licking each other.

***

"There's someone here for you", Bad Cop says. I can see he's not happy with that. They didn't even let us use the phone. Don't we have a right to a phone call? Bad Cop leaves the room and slams the door.

"You alright?", Caty asks.

"Yea, you?", I say.

"Pretty much", she says, "I keep worrying you're gonna say something. Don't say anything, actually. They're probably taping us right now."

I say nothing. The door opens.

"Hi gang", says Faust and puts his briefcase on the table.

"We're not a gang", I say. I'm slightly surprised. He's wearing a tie, as usual. And a gray suit. And rimmed glasses.

"Hi", says Caty, "thanks for coming."

"Sure, sure", Faust says, "let's make this quick. Have you said anything?"

"No", I say.

"No", Caty says.

"Great. Keep it that way. This room is tapped. Don't say a word until we've left. See you in a bit." He leaves his briefcase on the table and goes out to Bad Cop. He closes the door, so I can only hear muffled voices.

There's some calm explanation from Faust. Then angry screaming from Bad Cop. Faust's voice is completely flat, as if there's nothing at stake here. Whatever he's saying right now, Bad Cop is furious. He interrupts Faust and shouts again. Faust says a few words and Bad Cop stops shouting. Faust continues.

Two minutes later, they let us go.

"I didn't know you're an attorney", I say on the steps of the police building.

"Surprise", Faust says. He's carrying his briefcase.

"Thanks for getting us out", Caty says.

"Denton said you called him", Faust says, "you did the right thing, not saying anything. They got nothing on you. It isn't illegal to own twenty seven laptops."

"They said they were going to keep us for 24 hours or something", I say.

"The probably would, if they got anything out of you", Faust says, "but they have nothing."

***

"Take the next left", Faust says. I set the turning signal and the rental car crawls around the corner. There's a dark S-class limousine parked on the side of the road. Lights are off, or maybe the tinted glass doesn't let it through. I bring the car to a stop behind the Mercedes, then turn off the engine.

The left back door opens and Paul gets out of the car. He opens the trunk of the Mercedes and then walks up to us. Faust opens the passenger side door and Caty gets out of the back seat. We carry the laptops from the rental's trunk to the Mercedes in silence. Paul closes the trunk and holds out his hand.

"I'll take it back to the rental station", he says.

"Thanks", I say and drop the key in his hand.

"Daniel, pay the man", Caty says.

"Don't worry", Paul says, "that's included in the service."

"Service?", I say.

"The SRI", Paul says and gets in the rental.

"What is he talking about?", I say.

"Just get in the damn car", Caty says. The rental's wheels screech as Paul speeds off. I open the Merc's passenger door and get in the car. Denton's behind the wheel. Caty and Faust get in the back.

"What the hell's going on?", I ask Denton, "What's an SRI?"

"Second Realm Insurance", Denton says.

"Insurance? Against what?", I ask.

"Against the state", Denton says and starts the engine, "Second Realm businesses are in danger of being shut down by statists all the time. We're spreading out the risk by buying insurance against such a case. Like you just experienced." He moves the big car slowly.

"Wow", I say, "that's wicked."

"Thanks", Denton says.

"So how often do Second Realm businesses get shut down?", I ask.

"We were the first case", Caty says from the back seat.

"But I didn't buy any insurance", I say, "did you?"

"Michael did, as your employer", Denton says.

"Huh", I say, "that was smart of him, I guess."

"It was", Denton says.

"So when we get picked up by the cops, Faust comes and talks us out of it?", I ask.

"Don't make it a habit", Faust says.

"Your premium has increased", Denton says.

***

We drop Faust off in a fancy residential area and Denton drives on towards the business district. There's glass towers to each side of the street. It's a little like New York, but smaller. A few fast food restaurants and bars are still open. Hookers are standing on the street corners, waving as we cruise by. Finally, Denton pulls the Mercedes into an underground parking garage.

We enter the elevator. Caty yawns and leans her head against my shoulder. Denton enters a code in the elevator keypad and up we go.

"Where are we going?", I say.

The elevator stops and the doors open.

"This is my place", Denton says.

Pirate Bride
=============

We're standing in Denton's kitchen. It's huge. The counter tops are made of granite or marble or something else. The fridge and all the other appliances are brushed steel. They gleem in the fluorescent light as Denton offers us milk.

"I only have milk", he says and pours himself a glass, "you want some?"

"Sure", I say.

"I'd love to", says Caty.

"Hey, Denton", a female voice says from behind us, "did you bring some friends?"

I spin around. She's a vision. She's wearing only some skimpy white panties and a bra, but she doesn't seem very shy about her appearance. And why would she. She's almost as tall as I am in her bare feet. The low-hanging panties nicely reveal the muscles under the skin of her stomach and hips. There's a long scar across her stomach that draws all the way down into her panties. The way she's leaning against the doorway, legs casually crossed, she seems like out of an underwear ad. Her blond hair looks like she just got out of bed, in a very erotic way, all tossed up and fluffy. I suspect we might've interrupted her during some girl business.

"Oh, you're still up? We didn't mean to wake you, honey", Denton says. No way, THIS is his wife? Then again, who else would be in his penthouse in the middle of the night, wearing nothing but underwear?

"Hello", I say and wave shyly, "I'm Daniel."

"You can call me Lorelei", Lorelei says as she slowly strolls closer, each step deliberate and careful at the same time. Lorelei. In the future, everyone has a cool name.

"Hi", Caty says. She's grasping her glass of milk with both her hands. Her knuckles are white. If she grabs it any harder, she'll break the glass and cut her hands open.

"You must be Caty", Lorelei says, "Denton tells me all about you." No way. She really calls him Denton. I immediately wonder if she moans Oh, Denton! when they fuck. Does she know his real name? Does Denton even have a real name? Is there such a thing as a REAL name?

I drink some of my milk.

"So, what are you guys up to?", Lorelei asks.

"Not much, babe, we just got home from work", Denton says.

"You guys can crash in our living room if you want to", Lorelei offers, seeking eye contact. I try to maintain, but it's hard.

"Thanks", I say, evading her eyes. I look over to Caty, who's still clutching her milk. Her eyes are wide open and she's pressing her lips together. Her shoulders are slumped over.

"Hey Lor, can you entertain Daniel for a while? I want to show Caty my lab", Denton says.

"Sure", Lorelei says, "we'll pass the time."

Denton takes Caty's milk out of her hands and puts it on the counter top. Then he grabs her hand and pulls her into another room. Caty looks over her shoulder, staring at Lorelei.

"Sometimes he's such a nerd", Lorelei says and laughs. She opens a cabinet and pulls out a bottle of wine. She pours two glasses and sets them on the table.

"Your girlfriend doesn't talk much, does she?", Lorelei says.

"I'm not sure if she's my girlfriend", I say.

"Wine?", Lorelei says, offering me a glass.

"No thanks", I say. She puts the second glass on the counter next to Caty's milk. Then she lifts the wine glass to her lips and takes a sip. I watch her watch me as I watch her pour the wine into her mouth.

"You're not the elaborate type either, are you?", Lorelei says.

"I'm just stunned", I say. Lorelei laughs.

"Well, thank you, I guess", she says, "but your girlfriend-or-not isn't too bad either. So don't pretend like you're too stunned."

"Why are you married to Denton? I mean, he's a nice guy and all, but still", I say.

"Do you know anyone as cool as Denton?", Lorelei says.

"No", I say.

"Neither do I", says Lorelei.

"What's that on your stomach?", I ask.

Lorelei takes a sip of her wine. She looks down her body, as if contemplating the answer. She drops her free hand and slowly draws it along the length of the scar. She stops just shy of putting her hand down her panties. Then she sighs.

"The police", she says and takes another sip of wine.

"They beat you up?", I say.

"They broke down the door in the middle of the night", Lorelei says. "They were wearing full SWAT gear and automatic weapons. They threw a smoke grenade in the bedroom. I woke up coughing from Denton shouting for me to get under the bed."

"Did you get under the bed?", I ask.

"I didn't make it. I screamed as one of them hit Denton in the head with the butt of his MP5. He went down and they kicked him. I tried to get to him and they threw me down, too. And kicked me."

"Shit", I say.

"I was three months pregnant with my second child at the time", Lorelei says. She lifts the wine glass high and pours the rest of the wine into her lips. Then she sets the glass down on the counter. She leans back on the stone counter top, her elbows resting behind her slightly bent body. I stare at the long scar on her stomach.

"So did you..", I say.

"Take a look at the scar and have a guess", Lorelei says. I take another look at the scar, but I already knew the answer when I asked.

"Fuck", I say, "I'm really sorry."

"Don't be", she says.

"Why did they raid you in the first place?", I ask.

"One of Denton's clients was under suspicion of laundering money", she says, "at least that's their justification for killing my unborn child." She sounds bitter.

I don't know what to say, so I say nothing.

"When I got back from the hospital, I said: You can't stop now, Denton",
Lorelei says.

This is why Denton does all this. To make Lorelei happy. To make the
world a safe place for his family.

"Are you crying, mommy?", a little voice says from the doorway. A little
girl is standing there, a cushion in her arms that is almost as big as she is.

"No, honey, I'm alright", says Lorelei.

"Are you talking about my little brother?", says the girl.

"I don't know if he was a brother", Lorelei says, "but yes."

"It coulda been a brother", the girl says. Lorelei nods.

"Yes", she says to the girl, then, "aren't you sleepy?"

"I was, but then I heard you talk, and you sounded sad", says the girl, "I
don't want you to be sad. I brought you my cushion." She holds out the
cushion in front of her. Lorelei smiles.

"That's nice of you", she says to the girl. "Why don't you go back to your
room, and I'll be there in five minutes, ok? I'll just say goodnight to daddy's
friend. And give him a blanket. He's sleeping over."

"Daddy's having a sleepover?", the little girl says and smiles.

"Yes", Lorelei says, "he can tell you all about it tomorrow."

"You can have my cushion if you like", the girl says to me and sticks her
arms out, presenting the cushion to me.

"Thanks", I say, "but I think your mom might have another one. Thanks
though."

"I'll be in my room", says the little girl, "goodnight!"

"Night", I say and wave to her.

***

Lorelei has helped me pull out the couch and transform it into a bed. She has given me blankets and cushions. I thanked her and wished her a good night. I'm setting up the bedcouch when Caty comes into the room.

"Hey there", I say to her.

"Hey yourself", she says.

"How was Denton's lab?", I ask.

"It was good", Caty says.

"Anything I should see?", I ask.

"Hu? No, I mean- maybe. You should ask him yourself."

"What are you thinking about?", I ask.

"Denton's wife", Caty says.

"I'll be thinking about her when we're fucking next time", I say and giggle.

"That's extremely funny", Caty says.

"Oh, come on. You know what I'm talking about. She could be a model!", I say.

"Fuck you", Caty says. I say nothing. Caty is silent for a few seconds. Then she says: "I bet you didn't even recognize her."

"Recognize her? From where?", I ask.

"She's actually a model, you turd", Caty says, "or rather, she was a model."

"Oh", I say, "I didn't realize that."

"Of course you didn't, you two-dimensional ass", Caty says to me.

"Are you coming?", I ask and climb into the couch bed. I pat the extra cushion.

"You can have your own cushion", I say.

"That's superb", Caty says.

I say nothing and only look at her.

"So what did you and the beautiful Lorelei do while I was in the lab?", Caty asks.

"Not much", I say, "we talked."

"What did you talk about?"

"She told me about-", I hesitate. Maybe I shouldn't tell her this. "-a joke", I say, "she told me a joke."

"Tell it to me", Caty says and wiggles out of her pants, "I could use some cheering up."

"It wasn't funny", I say, "sorry." Caty sighs. She's standing there in her underwear and she's beautiful. She looks at me like she's not sure what to do with her life.

"I'm going to have a shit", Caty says and waits.

"Alright then", I say.

"Aren't you going to say something extremely funny about drugs?", she asks.

"Not tonight", I say.

Caty trods towards the bathroom and takes a dump with the door open. I hear her flush. She turns off the light and climbs into the bedcouch with me. Her body radiates heat and I feel her warmth beside me.

"Are you alright, Caty?", I ask.

"Not really", she says.

"I don't make fun of you, with the drugs and that. I worry about you", I say.

"Don't do that", she says, "you're not very good at it."

"Sorry", I say.

"You're not very good at apologizing either", she says.

"I really like you, ok? I might even love you. I don't want you to fuck yourself up. I like you now", I say.

"You like me? What a relief. I guess I can start feeling good about myself now", she says.

"Well, why don't you?"

She sighs.

"I thought if I threw myself hard enough at Denton, he would come to his senses and love me back", Caty says. It stings a little when she says "love".

"He has a wife and a little girl", I say.

"I realize that now. He's always talking about his oh-so-great-wife, but I hadn't really gotten that in my head. It was just his background, not really him, you know", she says. "And I understand now that he's not going to risk losing anything for me."

"Don't say that. He bailed us out of jail tonight, remember?"

"You know what I mean. He's not going to risk losing his supermodel wife and his daughter. Not for me."

I hug her under the blankets. Her thin body feels like molten steel in my arms.

"I think you're like a daughter for Denton", I say, "or maybe his little sister. He really likes you, just not, you know, in that way."

"I don't care about the other ways he likes me", Caty mumbles into her cushion.

"Do you care about the ways I like you?", I ask.

"At least you're relatively loyal", Caty says, "Danny the Dog."

"Whatever", I say, "I still like you. You're beautiful on the inside."

Caty laughs.

"How do you know what my inside looks like?", she says.

"You might not have realized this", I say, "but there's several orifices in your body. These allow a keen explorer to find out all about you."

"A keen observer", she says, chuckling, "what is this, a bad porn movie?"

"Something like that", I say, "are we going to fuck or what?"

"Fuck in Denton's living room? On his couch?", Caty says in pure delight, "serves him right."

"Don't make any stains", I say.

"Fuck that", Caty says, "I'm bringing the fire hydrant. Let's see how well his wife performs at basic household tasks. Laundry."

SmartMoney
==========

"I'm afraid there's not much of a breakfast", Lorelei says to us, "there's some cornflakes, I think." This morning she's wearing a loose shirt over her undies. Probably Denton's shirt. Why do girls always wear a guy's shirts as a trophy?

"Don't you eat breakfast?", I ask.

"Not here", Lorelei says, "I usually get some breakfast on the way back from the gym."

"Oh", I say, "you work out?"

"Yes", Lorelei says, "you think this thing maintains itself?" She gives herself a little clap on the butt.

"Maybe you should work out, Caty", I say.

"Fuck you", Caty says, "I have killer legs."

"That's true", I say. "Your's aren't bad either, Lor", I add.

"Thank you, Daniel", Lorelei says. "I'm going to get changed for the gym. Denton should be out any minute, I woke him up. Can't have the guests waiting all morning." She leaves the room.

"Thank you, Daniel", Caty says in a mocking voice.

"What? She's nice", I say.

"Let's eat her kid's cornflakes", Caty says and grabs the remaining milk from the fridge.

Caty has stuffed herself with the entire packet of cornflakes and drank the entire carton of milk when Denton finally joins us in the kitchen. He hands me a phone and gives one to Caty, too.

"Caty already knows what I'm talking about", Denton says, "but first let's get some breakfast."

***

I order eggs and bacon and guacamole.

"You're sick", Caty says, "there's something wrong with your brain."

"I like it", I say, "it tastes awesome on the eggs. And it cools them down faster."

"This isn't even a mexican restaurant", Caty says.

"They have guacamole on the menu", I say, "so why wouldn't I order it?"

"Because you're a reasonable human being", Caty says, "oh, wait."

"Quiet down, kids", Denton says, "I don't want to hear your bedroom talk." He pulls out his phone. It's the same as the one he gave me. I pull out mine. It's a Nexus S. Shiny. Denton starts an app on the phone. The waiter returns and brings coffee for Caty, an espresso for Denton and hot cocoa for me.

"Ok", he says, "this is how it works. Say you want to buy my espresso for 3€. But you don't want to use statist money, because you hate the state. What are you going to do?"

"Pay you in silver", I say.

"Great", Denton says, "do you have a 1/10th of an ounce coin with you?"

"I don't have any silver with me", I say, "but I could buy some from Caty."
I look at Caty, who's drinking from her cup.

"Do you have a 3€ silver coin?", Denton asks Caty.

"No", Caty says, "an ounce is about 31€ right now. Smallest coin I have is
half an ounce, so about 15.5€."

"So what do you do?", Denton asks me.

"I use my phone", I guess.

"Very good", Denton says and puts his phone on the table, "go ahead." I
pick up the Nexus S and swipe the screen to unlock it. There's an app on
the front page that is called SmartMoney. I open it. It gives me a list of
assets in the virtual wallet and the quantities in which I own them. I have 1
ounce of gold, 1 ounce of silver, $100, 100€ and 100BTC. I click "Pay".

"So should I give you euros? Or silver?", I ask.

"Doesn't matter", Denton says, "just pick any one of them." I pick silver. It
prompts me for the quantity. As I use the slider to select a tenth of an
ounce of silver, it shows me how much that is in the other assets I have. I
adjust it to 3.01€. Then I hit "Start transaction". The phone shows an image
of two phones held close together. The instructions read "Hold phone near
transaction partner's phone".

I put my phone next to Denton's phone on the table. They both show an
animation and then mine flashes "Paid 3.01€" and Denton's flashes
"Received 3.01€". Denton picks up his phone and puts it back in his
pocket. Then he pushes his espresso over to me.

"There you go", he says.

"I don't like coffee", I say.

"It's not coffee, it's espresso", he says.

"Espresso's still coffee", I say. Denton shakes his head.

"There IS something wrong with you", he says and takes his espresso back. He takes a sip and curses.

"Shit, this is hot. How can you drink it down like that?", he asks Caty.

"I'm like a porn star, I feel no pain in my mouth", Caty says.

"You young people make me crazy", Denton says and shakes his head. He takes a careful sip from his espresso. My eggs and bacon and guacamole arrives. Caty has ordered chocolate cake and Denton has buttered pretzels. I watch as Caty eats all of the chocolate from the top of her cake, then leaves the rest of it sitting on her plate. She leans back and holds her belly.

"I'm stuffed", she says, "this cake is really filling."

"Maybe it's the 500 grams of cereal you ate earlier with a liter of milk", I suggest.

"Now you're being unreasonable, Daniel", Caty says, "that was almost 30 minutes ago. That stuff went right through me." She cuts the cake into little pieces and drops them into her coffee, pushing them under with the spoon.

"People in Africa are starving right now", I say to Caty.

"I'd love to eat them", Caty says, "but I'm already full."

"You're wasting food", I say, "that cake could've fed 10 starving kids."

"Wasting food isn't the problem", Caty says, "it's just that the food over here doesn't help them in Africa very much."

"She's right", Denton said, "have you read Hernando de Soto's Mystery of Capital?"

"I haven't", I say, "I think you recommended it, but I haven't gotten around to it yet."

"The problem with third world country poverty isn't that we have food", Denton says, "it's their legal systems."

"Why, what's so bad about their legal systems?", I ask.

"It prevents the poor from enforcing their property claims", Denton says.

"You mean they get ripped off by the rich people?"

"Yes, through the government. The government enforces the property claims of politically connected or rich people, but forbids the poor from enforcing their own. They cannot build capital. Without capital, they can't escape poverty. In short, whenever they work, somebody takes their stuff away. Those people live in slums. They build a house, somebody throws them off the property. They save some money and buy tools, someone forbids them entry into the market. Somebody steals their money, the police laughs at them. They enforce their property rights themselves, the police throws them in prison. If they're lucky."

"So what can we do?", I ask.

"The answer, of course", says Denton, "is competing legal systems."

"Of course", I say.

"If you think about it", Caty says between drinking soggy coffeecake, "it isn't much different over here. The standard of living is just higher. But lots of people are prevented from market entry by stupid rules and regulations. Black market merchants can't go to the police. If they enforce their property rights themselves, they're criminialized."

"That's exactly right", Denton says.

"So you want to make it legal to compete with the government?", I ask.

"Fuck legal", Caty says with her mouth full, "make it possible."

"Caty brings up a great point", Denton says, "which is legality doesn't matter. As long as the state can just force us to do its bidding, what difference does it make if something is written on a piece of paper? They just ignore it."

"Is this related to your whole moral relativism thing?", I ask Caty.

"Kind of", she says, "legal and moral are both a fiction. If someone points a gun at you, it doesn't matter if you think he shouldn't be doing that. And it doesn't matter if you have a piece of paper saying he can't do it. He obviously can, and he does."

"Now Caty makes it sound very cynical and nihilistic", Denton says, "but it's actually a beautiful thing. It means you make your own freedom. Freedom isn't what someone else allows you. It isn't what someone else thinks you should be doing. Freedom means shaping reality the way you like it. Freedom is what you can do."

"So Caty is a nihilist and you're a constructivist", I say.

"Yes", Denton says, "and we're going to save the world."

***

"Now I'm not head of sales, that's Michael's job", Denton says, "but I need you to go to the US and propagate the WhisperPC."

"Wow", I say, "did you know about this?" I mean Caty.

"No", Caty says.

"You're going to do a little tour", Denton says, "I think you'll like it."

New Hampshire
===============

"BANG", the shotgun makes. The clay pigeon explodes into hundreds of shards and rains down to the earth. I remove my earmuffs.

"That was a nice shot", Bill says.

"Thanks", Caty says.

"You shot anything before?", Bill says.

"No", Caty says, "but I have a killer instinct. Hey Daniel, do you want to have a try?" She offers me the gun.

"Uh, sure", I say and take it. It feels heavy and clumsy in my hands. I'm careful not to point the bad end at anyone. I do the reloading motion, pulling the sled or whatever it's called back. It makes a nice chunky click sound and ejects the empty shell.

"Like this?", I ask, squinting my right eye.

"Yea", Bill says, "that's the way to do it."

"Try to time it with your breathing", Caty says.

Bill fires another clay pidgeon. I try to follow its arch with the rifle, but it's very heavy and sluggish. Nothing like Quake, really. When it starts to come down again, I aim in the general direction and pull the trigger. The rifle bangs and hits me in the shoulder.

"Fuck", I say, rubbing my shoulder, "that hurts."

"You're such a pussy", Caty says and laughs.

"Did I hit it?", I ask.

"Well", Bill says, being very diplomatic.

"No", Caty says.

"I'm not made for this", I say, "it's outdoors, it's in the fucking daylight. I'm a programmer. I'm not a savage like you people."

Caty rolls her eyes and grabs the rifle from me. She reloads and gives Bill a signal. They have already established some kind of primitive hunter-sign-language. This is ridiculous. The machine lobs another clay blob through the air in a high arch. I watch as Caty has one eye closed, tracing it for half a second before pulling the trigger. There's another loud bang and the recoil shakes her whole body. I'm thinking how the impact must hit her twice as hard as me, as she only has half the mass to absorb the shock. I don't need to look at the clay raining down to know she's hit it.

"Do you have anything besides buckshot?", Caty says.

"Now, you probably wouldn't hit a moving target at that distance with anything but spread", Bill says.

"I want to try", Caty says matter-of-factly. Bill shrugs and fumbles around in his pockets. He produces a small carton with ammunition labeled "Sabot". Caty pulls the shotgun action, ejecting the unfired round and catching it in her hand. She hands it to Bill and takes a slug from the carton.

"Now those aren't cheap", Bill says, "they're for extra precision and they fly faster. You will have to adjust for that."

Caty nods. I press my earmuffs against my head for extra protection. Caty gives Bill the thumbs up and Bill counts down from three. The clay pidgeon races through the air. As it reaches the peak of its arch, I hear a 'click' and then a loud boom. There's a fraction of a second in which nothing happens. Then the clay pidgeon explodes into pieces.

"Wow", Bill says. Caty smiles.

"I'm hiring you for personal protection", I say to Caty.

"I'm serious", Bill says, "that was a very difficult shot. You're talented."

"If only you knew", I sigh, "she is good at everything. Please stop feeding her ego."

***

"Oh, forget them", Bill says, "most of them are just a bunch of wannabe politicans and do-gooders. They're outright scared of associating with anything that might hurt their chances of getting elected."

"Not all of them, I hear", Caty says, "there seems to be a lot of civil disobedience going on, too." Bill grunts.

"Civil disobedience", he says and spits, "I call it being an idiot. Where's the use in spending your life in jail? That's not making anyone more free. Neither you nor anyone else. In fact, it costs me money if these morons go to jail. The state extorts more money from me to feed them."

"You pay taxes?", I ask.

"I was speaking hypothetically. Of course I don't pay taxes", Bill says.

"So they don't cost you anything", I say.

"You're technically correct", Bill says, "but I still think it's stupid."

"What about all the Ron Paul fans?", Caty asks.

"Don't get me started. Those clowns think if only Ron Paul was elected, everything would be great."

"You don't think he has a chance to become president?", I ask.

"That's not the point. Even if he got 100% of the votes, it wouldn't make a difference. You can't do the right thing - that's the point of the system. It doesn't help to be 'principled' or to know Austrian Economics or to wave the magic constitution. Until you show me bullet proof paper, I'm not counting on it for my safety."

"We're going to this PorcFest next week", I say.

"What the hell is a Porcfest?", Bill says, "it sounds nasty."

"It's where a lot of FSPers and other liberty people meet, it's right here in New Hampshire", I say, "you could come."

"Nah", Bill says, "you young people go and have Porcfests. I'm going to stay right here and do something productive with the precious time I have left."

"How old are you?", I ask.

"I'm 56", Bill says.

"You talk like you're going to die tomorrow. I'm guessing even with American medical technology, you'll live to at least 75", I say.

"Just wait until the government mandates old people be made into tires. I'm expecting it", Bill says.

"You're not even retired yet", I say, "they'll probably have better uses for you than making tires."

"Don't forget their economic calculation problem", Caty says, "even if there were a better use for Bill than making tires out of him, they wouldn't know about it."

"Let's get back to business, though. I'll take two", Bill says.

"Two?", I ask.

"One for tinkering around", Bill says, "and one for the business. That one should also have the VPN service."

"Ok", I say, "I'll get you another one from the car. Caty can fill you in on all the VPN details."

***

There's a buttload of people here. I hadn't expected that many. Hundreds of tents, stands, tables and shops. The porcupine is everywhere. Everyone and his dog has a yellow-black flag. Some say "Don't tread on me", some say "$", some say "A". One says "Agora! Anarchy! Action!". I like that one.

"I'm hungry", Caty says, "let's get something to eat."

"How can you be hungry again?", I say.

"I burn more energy. That's why I'm hot", she says and walks towards a booth. There's a sign saying "We take FRN, silver or barter items". I trod after her. The guy in the booth is busy making hamburgers and hot dogs. He smiles when Caty steps up.

"What can I do for you?", he says.

"You can feed me", Caty says.

"What do you like?", he says.

"Meat", Caty says.

"That's great", the guy says, "why don't you try a PorcBurger?"

"Is it made from Free Staters?", Caty asks.

"No", says the guy and laughs. He flips a burger and pulls another one out of the grill. He wants to put it on a bun, but Caty stops him.

"Just put it on a plate with some mustard", she says. He shrugs and hands her a paper plate with the hamburger, tomato slices and mustard.

"What do you want to pay with?", he asks.

"What do you take?", Caty asks.

"I probably take anything you got on you", the guys says. Caty laughs. She puts her hand in the pocket of her pants and pulls out a gold coin. She puts in on the counter.

"You got change for that?", she says.

"Uh", the guy says, "you got silver?" Caty puts the gold coin back in her pocket and fishes out a silver coin.

"That's still a bit much", she says, "you want to sell me 10 more burgers?"

"You can pay in Federal Reserve Notes", the guy says, "or I can give you Federal Reserve Notes back for that. What kind of coin is that, anyway? Haven't seen that one." He points to the silver coin.

"It's from Austria", Caty says, "It's called a philly. Listen." Oh oh, here comes the pitch. She pulls out her phone.

"Why don't I just pay you in SmartMoney? You can choose any currency you like and you'll have it in a few seconds. I can give you 3.1415925 grams of silver if you like, or BitCoins, or gold, or dollars, or whatever you want." Guy scratches his head.

"Using a phone?", he says, "I don't think my phone can do that."

"What kind of phone do you have?", Caty asks.

"iPhone", says Guy.

"Then there's an app for that", Caty says, "give it to me."

The guy pulls out his phone and hands it over. Caty taps the screen a few times and locates the SmartMoney app in the AppStore. She hands the phone back.

"Enter your password, install it, make an account, done. I'll be back in five minutes when I've eaten your burger", Caty says and takes her paper plate. The guy taps on his phone as we leave. Caty chomps on her burger and licks the mustard off of the plate.

"That was pretty smooth", I say, "you're a natural salesperson."

"Thanks", Caty says and smiles. When she's done with her burger, she crumples the paper plate and throws it on the ground.

"What'd you do that for?", I ask.

"Creating jobs", she says, "haven't you ever heard of the Broken Window Theory?"

"It's called Fallacy for a reason", I say.

"Oh, what did he know. He was French", Caty says.

***

"So you don't believe in any property at all?", Caty asks incredulous.

"No", the anarcho-communist says, "property is theft."

"If property is theft", Caty says, "what do you call it when I do this?" She takes a cookie from his cookie jar and puts in into her mouth.

"I call it sharing", he says.

"And this?" She puts both her hands into the jar and grabs as many cookies as she possibly can. One falls to the ground, she hugs the others to her chest.

"Now you're being disrespectful", he says.

"I thought you didn't like property", she says.

"Not disrespectful to me", he says, "to other people who might have a need for cookies."

"I have a great need for cookies", Caty says, "I'm the cookie monster." To some passerby she says: "Do you want to buy cookies? Only 50 cents!" One guy buys a cookie from her.

"Do you feel exploited yet?", I ask the guy.

"Kinda", he says, "that's not very nice."

"Wait until she doesn't pay you the full product of your labour", I say, "she can get mean sometimes."

"So really, when do you stop me? I have all your cookies. Can I take all your pamphlets? Your booth? Your toothbrush?", Caty asks. Then she eats a cookie, crunching it loudly.

"That wouldn't be property", he says, "that's possession."

"What's the difference?", I ask.

"Well, possession indicates that I am using it right now", he says.

"You're not using your toothbrush right now", Caty says and puts a cookie into her mouth.

"The reason why we reject the concept of property is absentee ownership", the anarcho-communist says.

"Like ownership of a toothbrush not currently in use?", Caty says.

"Technically, yes", he says, "but it's about using the state to enforce your so-called property. If you capitalists didn't have the power of the state at your disposal, you couldn't defend factories or unused land from the rightful owners."

"Uh oh", Caty says, eating a cookie with her mouth wide open, "he said the bad word."

"What word?", the guy says.

"Rightful", I say, "and rightful owners imply a concept of ownership, don't they?"

"The workers are doing all the work and are using the factory, so it's rightfully theirs", he says.

"How is that more right than absentee ownership by capitalist fat-cats?", I say.

"Cause the capitalist isn't doing any of the work", the ancom says.

"So?", I ask, "work gives you a right?"

"Yes, because you made it", he says.

"So if I made something and then left, why do I lose my right to it?", I ask.

"You no longer use it", he says.

"So if I put my fork down to take a drink, someone can rightfully take my food?"

"No, you have to wait a little. If you left your food on the table and it was still there the next day, you wouldn't be using it. So anybody could take it."

"I'm not doubting that anybody COULD take it", I say, "I'm doubting that your way is any more right than mine."

"What he's trying to say", Caty says, "is that the poor people are at fault for their poverty, for they leave the riches to the rich."

"Fucking Stirnerites", the ancom says, "can I have my cookies back?"

"All of them?", Caty asks, "I'm thinking some of them may have made their way into my poop." She drops the remaining cookies into the jar.

"You should totally come to our meetup tomorrow", the ancom says.

"We're leaving tonight", I say.

"Too bad", says the guy.

"I think you're wasting your time, by the way", says Caty, "I haven't seen any hardcore neo-lockeians or tea partiers. Nobody here's disputing that the currently rich are in some way or another subsidized by the state."

"Yea, you're right", he says, "most people are really ok. Most don't take ALL the cookies."

"Is it just because you hate money?", I ask.

"There's more to it", he says.

I take a cookie. It's pretty good, chocolate chip with macadamia.

"Thanks for the cookies", I say.

"You should read Kropotkin and Proudhon", the guy says.

"You think I haven't?", Caty says to him. He says nothing. We say goodbye and leave.

"Have you really read Proudhon?", I ask Caty.

"Of course", she says, "haven't you?"

"I tried, but he's really boring", I say. She shrugs.

"You did pretty well, Young Daniel", she says, "wax on, wax off."

"Fuck you", I say and smile.

Auburn, Alabama
==================

"And so it's really quite a beautiful thing", Tucker says on the stage.

"I'd do him", Caty says.

"You'd do everything", I say to her.

"You say that like it's a bad thing", Caty says.

"Shhh", someone makes in the row in front of us, turning back and looking angry, "I'm trying to listen to that!"

"Sorry", I mouth silently. Caty rolls her eyes and mouths "pussy" to me. I mouth "blow me" to her. She mouths "I will". Now I roll my eyes.

"You see", Tucker says on stage, "nobody forced or planned or organized this. The korean car factory was built because that best served the selfish interest of the korean car company. And they now provide thousands of new jobs in our town. Many of the people who were unemployed before, living off the government paychecks like drug addicts, have now taken control of their own lives. They work. They earn good money. They support themselves and their families. So what served the best interest of the korean car company also served the best interest of the people in town."

***

"Mr. Tucker!", Caty shouts. Jeffrey Tucker turns around and faces her. He's standing next to two other guys, but Caty knows no such thing as privacy or decency. She just shouts when she wants to. Then again, she's a hot girl in her twenties. The two guys are balding economists. She's not playing with a fair deck here. In fact I've never seen her play with a fair deck.

"Mr. Tucker, it's so great to finally meet you", Caty says, slightly out of breath. I'm suspecting she's faking the out-of-breathness to appear more erotic to Tucker. I've seen her sprint hundreds of meters and barely breathe. She's a fucking bicycle messenger.

"And you are..?", Tucker makes.

"Oh, excuse my manners, Mr. Tucker", Caty says, "I'm Catherine. This is my friend Daniel. We're fans. We came from Germany to see you."

"How flattering", Tucker says and smiles. He takes Caty's hand and bows deeply, kissing it. Then he shakes my hand. I shake it back. His handshake is firm, yet pleasant.

"Let me introduce you to my fine collegues, Mr. Douglas French and Mr. Walter Block", he says.

"Pleasure", French says and shakes my hand. He also shakes Caty's hand. No hand kiss. Same with Block.

"I'm an admirerer of your work on private roads, Mr. Block", Caty says.

"Thank you", Block says, "I didn't know we had such.. interesting readers."

"Oh, Mises.org is the rave in Germany", I say.

"We didn't mean to interrupt your conversation", Caty says, still fake-panting, "it's just that we've come all the way from Europe to get to know you, Mr. Tucker." Tucker looks at French, then at Block. Then back at Caty.

"I'll tell you something. We're on our way to lunch in a nearby restaurant. Why don't you join us?", he says.

"We'd love to", Caty says, all smiles. Tucker, quite the gentleman, opens the door for Caty. She giggles like a little girl. When the three Mises.org-guys are out of hearing range for a few seconds, Caty holds me back.

"Don't fail me, Daniel. You keep Block and French away from Tucker so I can venue-change and lay him. Okay?", she whispers.

"I thought you were my girlfriend and all", I say.

"Don't cockblock me", Caty says, "you know I LOVE economists."

***

We go to McDonalds. It's only a few hundreds meters from the Mises building. Restaurant. Yea, well.

"Ah, Mr. Tucker", says the McDonalds guy behind the counter, "so good to have you back!"

"Javier, my friend", Tucker says, "always a pleasure. We'd like a table for five, please."

"Of course, Mr. Tucker", says Javier, "why don't you sit over there in the corner next to the McCafe?"

"That's lovely", Tucker says. He then turns to us: "Is that alright with you?" I nod. Tucker turns back to Javier.

"What can you recommend today, Javier?", Tucker says, "It's a special occasion. We have guests from Germany."

"The Big Mac is always a good choice", Javier says, "or maybe the Veggie burger, if the young lady is a vegetarian."

"I'm not a vegetarian, Javier, I'm just skinny", says Caty, "I'll take the Big'n'Tasty menu with a large table water, please."

"A very good choice", says Javier and enters it into his computer terminal.

"I'll have a Big Mac and two hamburgers", I say.

"No menu?", Javier asks.

"No, thank you", I say. Javier nods. Doug French and Walter Block order their menus.

"Let me try the Spicy Grilled Cheese Chicken Burger", Tucker says.

"Of course, Mr. Tucker. Will you be enjoying the Hot'n'Fresh Coffee as usual?"

"I will, Javier", says Tucker, "thank you for remembering." Javier enters all our stuff into the terminal.

"That'll be $29.92", he says. I want to pull out my wallet, but Tucker signs me to put it back.

"You are my guests, all of you", he announces and pulls out a money clip. He takes out three tens and a five.

"Thank you, Javier", he says, "we'll be at our table." He puts the $35 on the counter. Javier puts $30 into the register and $5 into his pocket.

"Thank you very much, Mr. Tucker. I'll be right over with your order.

"Did you just tip the cashier at McDonalds?", I ask Tucker.

"Yes, I did", Tucker says, "I love the service in this place. And the atmosphere. It's quite excellent. Have a look at the leather." We sit down in the corner. There's actually leather on the bench. Tucker makes the strategic error of sliding into the bench first. Caty immediately slips past me and slides in next to him. I remember my duty and sit on a chair in such a way that French and Block are blocked from Tucker. I'm blocking Block. Heh.

"So how did you get interested in Austrian economics?", French asks.

"It started with the financial crisis", I say, "I suddenly realized that mainstream economists seemed to have no clue what they were talking about."

Javier comes with our food. I chomp into my burgers. Caty is sweettalking Tucker to my left and I realize I must put on my best Austrian game to distract these two from her. Block is already sneaking looks at her. I suspect their knowledge of markets is vastly superior to mine, so I'll have to drag them down the moral road.

"Mr. Block", I say, "I've read your 'Defending the Undefendables' and must disagree with you on a few very important points."

Block looks at me.

"Like what?", he says. Time to wing it.

"One of the basic premises is that prostitutes, pimps, drug dealers, slumlords and speculators are heroes. You define a hero as someone who goes to at least moderate personal risk in order to fulfill the desires of other market participants, while not violating any moral principles himself."

"Yes. Which part do you disagree with?", Block asks.

"I challenge the very notion of 'moral'", I say. Block exchanges looks with French.

"Look", he says, "what I base the definition of 'moral' on is the NAP, or the Non-Aggression-Principle. It-"

"I understand the Non-Aggression-Principle", I say, "but I don't see how that gives you a non-arbitrary definition of 'moral'. The whole natural rights theory is nothing but a huge fallacy."

"You don't think that every human has the right not to be aggressed against?", French asks and raises his eyebrows.

"Oh, I do think that. But I think you can't prove it", I say. Ha. Now I've got them both. I can hear Caty laughing and giggling and doing her warmup routine on Tucker.

"Then why do you believe it?", French says.

"I just do, no reason", I say.

"Murray Rothbard, in 'The Ethics of Liberty', proves-", starts French, but I interrupt him.

"Let's say 'states', Mr. French", I say, "'proves' is a bit much."

"Alright. He states that every human being has the inherent right to life, liberty and the property he rightfully makes his own by mixing his labor with unused natural resources or by voluntary trade", French says.

"Let me stop you right there", I say, "why only humans?"

"What?", Block says.

"Why do only humans have inherent rights?"

"Are you a vegan?", French asks.

"No", I say, "I just ate three burgers. But I find it arbitrary to exclude animals."

"Animals can't reason, and thus are not capable of grasping the concept of rights or law", says French.

"Say you", I say, "have you asked any animals?"

"No", French says, "they can't speak. That's why they don't have any rights."

"So do french people have rights?", I say, "I can't understand a word they're saying."

"They just speak a different language", French says.

"So do animals", I say.

"Animals don't have the capability to reason", he says.

"That seems quite arbitrary a judgement to base your entire concept of rights upon", I say.

"What do you mean, arbitrary?", French asks.

"You, as a human, say: I, as a human, have rights, because I can reason. Non-humans can't reason. Therefore they don't have rights."

"Yes", he says.

"That's basically the rascist argument. I, as a white man, have rights, because I am white. Non-whites aren't white. Therefore they don't have rights."

"That's completely different", French says.
I realize that Caty and Tucker are gone. I can't turn now, or Block and French will realize, too.

"It's a different judgement, but it's the same principle", I say, "you give yourself rights based on your uniqueness, which also gives you the right to deny other creatures said rights. It's just an euphemism for 'I'm special, so I can kill others'."

"So why do you eat animals then?", French says.

"Because I'm special", I say, "but I don't use an euphemism."

"Natural rights theory isn't the only argument for the Non-Aggression-Principle", Block says, "are you familiar with Hans-Hermann Hoppe?"

"I'm familiar with his ethics, and I think they're full of fail", I say. Block and French exchange looks.

***

"The principle of first ownership", I say, "that's great. It's such a logical circle it isn't even funny."

"How is it a circle?", Block asks.

"Why don't you make the argument, and I'll take it apart for you", I say.

"Hoppe states that the first person to claim an unused part of land, resource or whatever - even your own body - is the rightful owner. If it was, say, the last person to claim, then the person after him would be the rightful owner, then the person after him, and so on."

"You imply the conclusion right there", I say, "you assume that there must be some type of exclusive property in everything. Why must there be property at all?"

"Well, there-", Block starts.

"Secondly, why not the last person? Just because it would be silly? Owners would change all the time, but that doesn't prove anything. Just because you don't like or can't imagine the implications of the last claimant being the legitimate property owner, that doesn't prove it must be the first."

***

"In his argumentation ethics", Block says, "Hoppe explains how the very fact that one is able to discuss rights theory is proof of rights in and of themselves."

"How's that?", I ask.

"In order to argue, one must have possession of his own body. Therefore, someone claiming 'there are no rights', is making use of said rights, contradicting himself. Hoppe calls this a performative contradiction."

"It's bullshit", I say, "come on. First, I don't need to be completely free in order to argue. In fact, I bet most people in prison argue all day long, and they're not free."

"They're in control of their own bodies", Block says.

"But they're behind bars. Second, the very fact that a performative contradiction can happen is proof to me that there are no rights."

"How do you mean?", Block asks.

"Hoppe claims that there is some objective moral ethic everyone should act by - a right. Yet obviously it is possible for people to ignore this rule. So why bother with it? If it exists, it doesn't mean much if people can just break it. The law of gravity would be an interesting subject for a performative contradiction. It works, even if people don't believe in it. An objective law or right that only works if people agree with you is completely worthless."

"Hmm", Block says.

"Hey, where's Tucker?", French says.

***

"So how was he?", I ask Caty.

"Oh, shut up", she says.

"What? Didn't you bang him?", I say. It's funny now, because I know she didn't.

"He wouldn't stop talking. We drank lots of whiskey and I thought he was getting loose, but he just kept telling me stories and how I reminded him of all those other people", she says.

"Maybe he thought you were too young", I say.

"Daniel, you don't understand how men work. Older men love me. I'm attentive. I listen to their crap. I admire them. And I'm fucking hot", she says.

"So why not Tucker?", I ask.

"I don't know. In the end I went so aggressive he couldn't have missed it. But he did. It's like he has cognitive dissonance. I was literally sitting in his lap, hugging him and licking his face."

"Maybe he doesn't like to be licked. Isn't he a devout christian?", I ask.

"They all are", Caty sighs, "they all are."

"Maybe you're mentally ill", I say, "you like people who don't like you."

"He liked me", she says.

"Who don't want to fuck you", I correct myself.

"You could be right", she says and sighs again.

"Did you try Marie on him?", I say cautiously.

"What? No!", Caty says, "Marie is only for you. You know that."

***

"So, economically speaking, a state-based society would have a far weaker defense than a free-market-based society with competing defending agencies", Robert P. Murphy says into the microphone.

"Now of course some people will argue", he continues, "that three ancaps with guns wouldn't have stopped Hitler's army." Everybody laughs. Especially Caty. She's so into this guy. I should be an economist.

"I give them that", Murphy says, "but France had a state. They had an army. That didn't help them, now did it." Laughter.

"My argument is not that a free-market defense is invincible", he says, "it is merely that, given the same resources, people and otherwise the exact same circumstances, a free-market defense will be more efficient and more effective than a state monopoly. Thank you very much."

Applause. He takes questions. A microphone goes around.

"Dr. Murphy, I'm playing the devils advocate here. Wouldn't competing defense agencies wage war against each other? If Smith was insured by Defense, Inc. and Jones was insured by SHIELD, why would Jones obey an insurance claim by Smith? He could just announce that he doesn't recognize the claim and send SHIELD after Smith and Smith's defense agency, Defense Inc."

"That's a common question", Murphy says, "and there are many answers. For example, most customers probably wouldn't want their defense agencies waging war against other's. Wars are expensive. The premiums would go up. Customers would leave. Wars kill people. Nobody wants to be killed because someone's TV was stolen. Or because someone stole his TV. So the incentives of the market work in such a way as to reward an efficient, peaceful solution. A defense agency that waged war all the time would also have a hard time attracting personnel. Try hiring people if the chance to get shot on the job is 10% and the same job somewhere else has only 0.01% chance of getting you shot."

The microphone gets passed around. Caty leans forward and snatches it from some dude who was going to ask a question. She stands up and breathes into the microphone excitedly.

"Dr. Murphy", Caty asks, "do you want to go for a drink with me later?"

"That's also a very common question", Murphy says. Laughter. He IS funny.

TAZ
===

I'm nervous at the customs check, even though we don't have anything illegal on us.

"How was your .. vacation?", the customs agent asks me.

"Very relaxing", I say, "if only it wasn't over!" He laughs.

"Yea, don't we all wish vacation was never over", he says. We do look a bit like tourists. No luggage but backpacks, t-shirts, shorts. Caty's wearing huge sunglasses that she bought for $5 at PorcFest. She looks extremely tanned, but that's just her natural complexion. Even I have a little tan on me. We could be backpackers, I guess.

"Welcome to Germany", the customs man says and waves us through. Caty reaches into her pocket and pulls out her A-phone. She reads something, then turns to me.

"They're meeting us outside", she says.

"Cool", I say.

"Cooler than you think", Caty says.

"What's that supposed to mean?"

"You'll see", she says.

***

Outside, I immediately see Denton's Mercedes S-Class. He's parked exactly in the middle of the no-parking-zone. It's only a few steps from outside the terminal door to the car. People probably think the dark limousine belongs to some kind of diplomat or politician. Nobody would dare to park so criminally offensive if he wasn't allowed to. Or maybe Denton actually pulled some strings to get a license to park there. Who knows.

"Welcome back", Denton says when I get in the car. He's in the back seat. Paul's driving, Faust's in the passenger seat. I sit behind Faust and Caty throws her backpack in and climbs over me, sitting between Denton and me. He gives her a hug and then tells her to put her seatbelt on.

"Paul's driving", he says. "You never know what happens."

"Oh, come on", Paul says, "I'm a very calm driver."

"What about that A4 earlier?", Faust says.

"He was asking for it", Paul says, "who drives 50 in a 50 zone? That's just ridiculous."

"How was your trip?", Faust asks.

"It was awesome", I say, "we met Bill, and we went to PorcFest, and we went to the Mises Circle, and.."

"And we sold thirty WhisperPCs and fifty SmartMoney apps. Mostly to gatekeepers and trendsetters", Caty says.

"That's what I like to hear", Denton says.

"Where's Michael?", I ask.

"He's at the TAZ", Paul says.

"Shhh", Faust says.

"The TAZ?", I ask "you're not talking about the Tageszeitung, are you?"

"It's a surprise", Caty says and smiles.

"Great", I say, "everybody knows about it but me."

"You'll be more surprised", Denton says.

***

"No fucking way", I say.

"Fucking way", Michael says. He's beaming. My mouth hangs open.

"The entire top floor?", I ask.

"The entire two top floors", Michael says and smiles.

"That's not really a TAZ any more, that's a PAZ", I say, "well, at least I hope the A part is true."

"It's pretty autonomous", Michael says, "we made sure of that."

We're riding up the elevator in what is probably one of Berlin's highest skyscrapers in the business district. The doors open with a ching-ching sound and I see the lobby. It's massive. There's sofas to lounge around in, pleasant, yet unobtrusive music playing. There's a reception desk with a pretty woman behind it. She looks very professional. So does her smile.

"Mr. Myers", she says and smiles a lot. Michael introduces Caty and me. I shake her hand. The two floors are broken up in the lobby and I can see what looks like office rows. There's a lot of open space and glass panels. Michael leads us up the stars.

"These are our offices", he says. His says M. Myers, CEO. Then there's J.C. Denton, CTO. The two offices are connected. Then there's a bigger office space with a few desks in it. H. Faust, P. Allen, C. Callahan and N.M. Realname.

"Callahan? Young, thin Caty Callahan?", I say to Caty. She smiles. "The receptionist won't stop laughing when people call us", I say.

"I don't mind", Michael says, "she has a very sexy laugh."

"You guys just want a receptionist so you can get laid at the office!", I complain.

Michael smiles.

"You say it like it's a bad thing", he says.

I sit at my new desk. I have a sophisticated chair with several levers and knobs that I don't understand at all. I pull some, press others, and completely fuck up the settings. Caty takes a running start, jumps into her chair and rolls it the entire length of the office.

"Sweet!", she shouts.

Then she hits the back wall with her chair and falls off.

"This is a pretty damn nice office or five", I say. "Did you rob a bank or something?"

"Business is great", Denton says, "the more states fuck up, the more customers we get to serve."

"And the more customers we serve, the less money states get to steal from them", Michael says, "so they fuck up more."

"I call it the vicious cycle of liberty", Paul says.

"Are you saying we're like a virus?", I ask.

"Yes", Paul says.

"Maybe we shouldn't put that into our marketing material", I say.

"Maybe we already thought of that", Michael says.

"Maybe", I say.

"Plus it's the good kind of virus. The kind that calls for your birthday and never forgets to flush the toilet", Paul says.

"So we won?", I ask. Denton laughs.

"We haven't won everything", he says, "but we've reached the next level. And we're on a winning streak."

My phone rings. I lean forward in my complicated chair and pick it up.

"Hello?", I say.

"Take your time", Caty says on the phone, "think about your next breath."

"Who is this?", I ask and smile.

"I'd like to book a date with one insanely hot C. Callahan", Caty says.

"She's so high, she's never coming down", I say into the phone, "can I interest you in a multi-hop VPN anonymizer?"

"That sounds kinky", she says and breathes loudly into the phone.

"Don't call here anymore", I say, "this is a serious business."

***

"I'm going to check if my apartment is still there", Caty says.

"You think it left?", I ask.

"I think someone may have homesteaded it", Caty says.

"See you later?", I say.

"Can't you sleep without me for one night?", Caty says, "You're suffocating me. I need more space. I want a divorce. You take the children."

"Breakfast?", I say.

"Sure", Caty says.

I call our receptionist with my A-phone to have her find the closest hotel.

"Regular or Second Realm?", she asks.

"What's closer?", I ask.

"There's a very nice Second Realm hotel just a few minutes up on Friedrichsstrasse", she says and gives me the address.

I'm amazed at how well hidden the hotel is. Standing in the lobby of the building, I wouldn't know there's rooms to rent in it if I hadn't been told. In fact, I'm not sure I'm in the right building. I open the Hotel app on my phone and book a room. They're 15€/night in this locale. I pay in gold backings from my Open Transactions account. Somewhere in the darkness, a green LED lights up. I find a small PO box with a key in it. It's labeled "12th floor, room 1203". I enter the elevator and go up to my room. Luxurious, to say the least. After taking a shower and looking out of the window over the city, I go to bed.

Agora

=====

I wake up when the phone rings. It's the receptionist relaying a message from Caty. "Where the FUCK are you", she reads me and wishes me a good morning. I text Caty that I'll be there in 30 minutes and get up.

From: Tom <tom@moriartyconsulting.com>
To: Daniel <dan@skynet.com>

Subject: 2 girls 1 cup

hey dan the man WHAT IS UP!

hope you're doing well. i just passed the 30.000€ mark. of course i don't keep it in euros. i don't get paid in euros, either. at least not often. DCs for the win! got the shit all locked away in shares and futures not traceable to me. may the apocalypse come. how's your grrrlfriend doing? tell her to blow me.

tom

*You have joined #agora
Michael: yea its pretty sweet. if youre in berlin some time check it out. you can even get a 2nd realm room close by.
daniel: i'm in such a room close by right now, haha
Michael: friedrichstrasse?
daniel: yes it's steep at 50/night but hey its like 5 star
Fellow Traveler: Check out the new OT client
http://orlingrabbe.com/?p=1476084340
daniel: sweet
Michael: looking good
nick_otc: anyone selling bitcoin? will pay $40/btc
Denton: when it's done, we can put it on the new WhisperPC as the default payment client. model 2.0 is going to be big. and cheaper. love economies of scale!
Fellow Traveler: Some guy in Singapore is building an OT bank
Michael: yea we have an investor who wants to build a 2nd TAZ in hamburg
Fellow Traveler: Cool. I'll definitely visit you guys when I'm in Germany again.
*C4ty has joined #agora
daniel: SHIT i gots to go! cya guys later!
C4ty: WHERE ARE YOU DANIEL? ALL WORK AND NO PLAY MAKES CATY A DULL GIRL
daniel: on my way sry
*You have left #agora

***

"Hey", I say to Caty.

"'Hey', he says", Caty says.
"I'm sorry", I say.

"You said breakfast", she takes a look at an imaginary watch on her wrist, "it's almost twelve!"

"I know", I say, "I'm sorry."

"You better make this up to me", she says.

"How?", I ask.

"I don't know. Why do I have to do all the work? You're late, so YOU come up with the making up!"

"I'll think of something", I say.

"I ordered lunch for us", she says.

"I thought we said breakfast", I say.

"Don't overdo it", she says, "I have limits."

"I haven't seen them", I say. She smiles.

"That was sweet", she says.

"Are we even?", I ask.

"Of course not. I've been waiting for over an hour. You can't just sweettalk your way out of this, Mister", she says and pouts.

"So what's next?", I ask, "I got the girl, I got the money, I got the office. What's left? World domination?"

"I'm not so much into the whole domination thing", Caty says, "I think."

"What do you have in mind?", I ask.

"Let's do world liberation. Imagine if just 10% of all people had the freedom we have", Caty says.

"Why do you people always have to save the world?", I ask. Caty shrugs.
"I guess it comes with the job if you're right about everything", she says.

"Just for the record: you're NOT right about everything", I say.

"Oh yea? Name a single thing I was wrong about, ever", she says.
I don't remember anything on the fly.

"I don't know, but there has to be something. I know it. Nobody's right about everything", I say.

"Except superheroes", Caty says.

"You're NOT a superhero", I say.

"Are you sure?", she says.

I eat a shitload of scrambled eggs and bacon and guacamole. Caty drinks burning hot coffee that doesn't even affect her. Maybe she IS a superhero.

"That'll be 21.50€", the waitress says. I search for my wallet. Shit. Nothing in the left pocket, nothing in the right pocket, just my phone in the jacket. The waitress eyes my phone and leans closer.

"If you prefer", she whispers, "we also take SmartMoney."

Caty smiles.

***

"See you later, alligator", I say to Caty.

"In a while, crocodile", she says. She dons her messenger bag and gets on her bicycle. She hops around a bit, then gets off the saddle and leans over to me. She gives me a big kiss on the cheek.

"Go ahead and bang hookers", she says, "while Caty goes and earns some money."

She puts her feet into the pedal straps and races off. Her bag jumps up and down, dancing on her hip. There she goes. I check the time on my phone. It's 13:37 on a sunny Wednesday. There's liberty to be built.

What do I do next?

Get Shane Radliff's book and learn about alternative lifestyles in pursuance of freedom!

VONU
A Strategy for Self-Liberation
by Shane Radliff

LIBERTY UNDER ATTACK PUBLICATIONS